ALSO BY DAN GUTMAN

The Get Rich Quick Club

Johnny Hangtime

Casey Back at Bat

Rappy the Raptor

Baseball Card Adventures

Honus & Me   *Satch & Me*

Jackie & Me   *Jim & Me*

Babe & Me   *Ray & Me*

Shoeless Joe & Me   *Roberto & Me*

Mickey & Me   *Ted & Me*

Abner & Me   *Willie & Me*

The Genius Files

Mission Unstoppable   *You Only Die Twice*

Never Say Genius   *From Texas with Love*

License to Thrill

**And don't miss any of the books in the
My Weird School, My Weird School Daze,
My Weirder School, and My Weirdest School series!**

DAN GUTMAN

FLASHBACK FOUR
FOUR
THE POMPEII DISASTER

HARPER
An Imprint of HarperCollinsPublishers

The author would like to acknowledge the following for use of photographs:
Travis Commeau, 45; Nina Wallace, 61, 74, 114, 237

ISBN 978-0-06-237444-8

Typography by Carla Weise
18 19 20 21 22   CG/LSCH   10 9 8 7 6 5 4 3 2 1
❖
First Edition

TO NINA, SAM, AND EMMA

Special thanks to the people who helped me with this project: Rosemary Brosnan, Lello Coppola, Melanie Weil Goldman, Andrew Eliopulos, Alan Kors, David Lubar, Kelly Eckel Mahoney, Ellen Graff Roberts, Liza Voges, Nina Wallace, and Allen Winningham.

You could hear the shrieks of women, the wailing of infants, and the shouting of men; some were calling their parents, others their children or their wives, trying to recognize them by their voices. People bewailed their own fate or that of their relatives, and there were some who prayed for death in their terror of dying. Many besought the aid of the gods, but still more imagined there were no gods left, and that the universe was plunged into eternal darkness for evermore.

—*seventeen-year-old Pliny the Younger,*
eyewitness to the eruption of Mount Vesuvius

INTRODUCTION

EVERY STORY SHOULD START WITH A BANG. THIS one starts off with just about the biggest bang ever.

The date: August 24, 79. That's not 1979. It's not 1879 either. It's the year 79. In other words, our story takes place seventy-nine years after they started counting years. It was a *long* time ago.

The place: the city of Pompeii, on what is now the west coast of Italy.

Picture this: It was nine o'clock on Tuesday, like any other Tuesday morning during the Roman Empire. Merchants were working in their shops, and farmers in their fields. Children were playing.

Pompeii was a bustling town with twenty thousand people. Everybody was going about their business, living their lives. It was a hot day, like most summer days in Pompeii.

Few people noticed anything different at first, but the birds had stopped singing. Dogs became agitated, and they started to howl. The cattle were moaning. Animals have some kind of a sixth sense. They know when something terrible is about to happen.

Ordinarily, I don't like to describe the weather in books. You know how some authors try to set the "mood" and go on for page after page talking about what the sky looks like, or the shape of the clouds?

My attitude is, who cares? Weather is boring. It bogs down the story.

But in this case, I'm going to make an exception. In this story, the sky and the clouds matter.

The waters around the Bay of Naples near Pompeii had suddenly become choppy. There was a chill in the air, and an eerie silence.

Ten miles northwest of Pompeii is a large hump-backed mountain—Mount Vesuvius. It's a little over four thousand feet high, with green forests on its slopes. Oh, and it's also a volcano. That's important.

People had felt a few minor tremors around Vesuvius over the previous four days. But the mountain hadn't erupted for hundreds of years, so nobody was overly concerned.

Just after nine o'clock in the morning, a thin line of steam rose out the top of Vesuvius. A small amount of ash spit out and sprayed like a fine mist on the eastern slope of the mountain. People in Pompeii and the neighboring towns barely noticed.

But around noon, the ground started to vibrate in Pompeii. Some tiles were shaken off roofs. They shattered as they hit the ground.

And then, suddenly, Vesuvius blew its top! The peak of the mountain *exploded* like the cork out of a bottle. Molten rock and pumice blasted out of Vesuvius, mixed with ash and gas—a million and a half tons of debris per second. It was like an atomic bomb, but bigger. People who were hundreds of miles away could hear it. There was a giant crater where the top of Mount Vesuvius had been.

In Pompeii, the people stopped what they were doing and stared at Vesuvius in the distance. The smart ones gathered up their belongings and made a run for it. They headed for the Bay of Naples to board boats and get out of there.

The boiling rock shot high in the sky. Within a half hour, a dense mushroom-shaped cloud had risen ten miles above Vesuvius. It would eventually reach a height of twenty miles. And the wind was blowing that cloud toward Pompeii.

Then the debris began to spread out, mix with cold air in the atmosphere, and solidify. The sky turned dark. By three o'clock, the sun was blocked out. It looked like nighttime in the middle of the afternoon. The mushroom cloud collapsed, and all that stuff that had blasted out of the mountain started falling from the sky.

Rocks rained down like hot, black snow. Some were as small as golf balls. Others were as large as watermelons. They hit the ground like missiles, slamming into houses and killing people instantly. Families dashed for shelter or helped the wounded and dying. Bricks, tiles, stones, and junk were flying everywhere. People climbed trees. Animals ran around crazily. The ground was shaking. Buildings were crushed. People were screaming. Hot ash was falling like snow, and in an hour there were five or six inches on the ground, covering Pompeii. It looked like the end of the world.

More people tried to flee the city at this point.

Thousands escaped. The rest figured it would all blow over, and life would return to normal. Big mistake.

It wasn't a constant bombardment of debris that spewed out of Mount Vesuvius. It came in surges. There was another one at five thirty. Sparks flew, and lightning flashed in the sky. Buildings shook, collapsed, and caught on fire. Bigger pieces of rock were falling from above, destroying everything they landed on. Roofs that were only designed to withstand rain caved in from the weight, wiping out entire families. The devastation was incredible. Even the course of the River Sarno had changed. Two feet of ash and stone covered the ground now.

By evening, things had calmed down. Rocks and boulders were no longer falling from the sky, but fires were burning everywhere. First-story doors and windows were covered by five feet of ash.

The survivors probably thought they had lived through the worst of it when they went to bed that night. They were wrong. Vesuvius wasn't finished yet. The worst was yet to come.

At six thirty the next morning—August 25—there was *another* surge of volcanic activity. A glowing cloud spilled over from the top of Mount Vesuvius and began to roll down the sides of the mountain.

It wasn't lava. Lava moves slowly, and can be avoided. This was a gigantic wave of toxic sulfuric gas mixed with hot cinders and pieces of molten rock. It was moving fast, close to a hundred and eighty miles per hour. And it was *hot*, maybe seven hundred degrees. It poured into Pompeii like a hurricane and enveloped it, incinerating everything in its path. A black cloud of death.

If you wanted to say something positive about the destruction of Pompeii, you could say the people who were still alive at that point didn't suffer much pain. In fact, they might have been the lucky ones. Death was almost instantaneous.

Then there was an eerie silence. It was over. The sun tried to poke through the dust and smoke, but it was a lost cause. The sky would be dark for the next three days. There were no cries for help. Nobody was left alive. A gray haze hung over everything.

In less than twenty-four hours, the city of Pompeii and its two thousand people had been buried under a ten-billion-ton mountain of ash.

It was like Pompeii had never even been there.

STUCK IN THE PAST

TO TELL THIS STORY THE RIGHT WAY, WE NEED TO go back, or, I should say, *forward* in time. Specifically, we need to go to April 18, 1912.

Pretend you're watching a movie in your head. It was a cold and rainy day. Okay, okay, no more weather, I promise! It doesn't matter anymore.

This part of the story takes place in New York City. Remember, this is forty years before the Empire State Building was built. New York is still a big city, but the skyscrapers haven't gone up yet.

Now zoom in. You're looking at Pier 54, near

Fourteenth Street, at the edge of the Hudson River. Can you see the park bench near the water? There are four kids sitting on that bench. Sixth graders. Two girls, and two boys—Luke, Isabel, Julia, and David. They call themselves the Flashback Four.

Of course, you already met these kids if you read *Flashback Four: The Lincoln Project* and *Flashback Four: The Titanic Mission.* If you haven't read those books, you really need to. If you *have* read them, you're ahead of the game.

Luke, Isabel, Julia, and David were not *supposed* to be in New York City in the year 1912. It was all a huge mistake. What had happened was that a Boston billionaire named Chris Zandergoth—or "Miss Z," as she is called—used her fortune to develop a smartboard much like the ones in your school, except that it also functions as a time-traveling device. Miss Z has a special interest in collecting photographs of things that have never been photographed before. So she recruited the Flashback Four and assigned them to go back to 1912 to take a picture of the *Titanic* as it was sinking. Her intention is to build a museum filled with photos of great moments in history.

Well, the kids did take the picture, but due to

circumstances beyond their control, they were unable to get back to their own time before the *Titanic* went under. After a terrifying dip in the frigid Atlantic, where they very nearly drowned, Luke, Julia, Isabel, and David managed to climb aboard a lifeboat. Along with nearly seven hundred other *Titanic* passengers, they were rescued by a ship called the *Carpathia*. It steamed into New York Harbor a few days later. And that takes us up to where we are now, with the Flashback Four sitting on a bench near the water. The wind blew a newspaper across the pier. . . .

If you want to learn more about what happened on the *Titanic*, read *Flashback Four: The Titanic Mission*. I don't have time to tell that story now. I've got *another* story to tell.

So these four kids are sitting on the bench that you're looking at in your mind's eye. The crush of reporters, photographers, and loved ones who had greeted the *Titanic* survivors is over. They all went home. The Flashback Four sat on Pier 54 and stared across the water at the shores of New Jersey.

"I'm hungry," said Luke, a big boy who was pretty much always hungry.

"How can you think about food at a time like this?" snapped Isabel. "My whole life is over."

Isabel's life was *not* really over, and in fact, her life would be starting all over *again*, except in the year 1912. She wiped a tear on her sleeve.

An hour before, the kids had still held out the faint hope that Miss Z or her assistant, Mrs. Vader, would be waiting at the pier to scoop them up and transport them back home to Boston in the twenty-first century. But those hopes dwindled as the pier gradually emptied. There would be no rescue this time. They were alone. It was starting to sink in that they would have to spend the rest of their lives in the wrong century. All four of them were tired, miserable, and still in a state of shock.

"I'll never see my family again," mumbled David, the only African American in the group. "I'll never see my dogs again."

At the mention of family and pets, Isabel and Julia burst into tears.

By all rights, this is where the time-traveling adventures of the Flashback Four should come to an end. They're stuck. There's no way out.

But obviously, that can't happen. We're only at the beginning of the book. You're only on page 11. If our story ended here, it would be a short story, not a book.

Something, of course, will have to happen. Please be patient.

"It wasn't supposed to go this way," Isabel moaned through her tears. "What went wrong? I'm the good kid. I always did everything I was told to do. Why me? What am I going to do *now*?"

David and Julia just shook their heads.

It's been said that people who have suffered a traumatic experience go through five stages of grief—denial, anger, bargaining, depression, and finally acceptance. The Flashback Four were churning through those stages quickly.

"Look on the bright side," Luke told the others. "Fifteen hundred passengers on the *Titanic* died. We didn't. We survived. That's a *good* thing, right? We'll just have to start over again."

"Luke's right," Julia said, getting up off the bench. "Our lives aren't over. Maybe they're just beginning."

Isabel and David were not convinced. They hung their heads forlornly.

"Think of it this way," Luke told them. "Nothing worse than this will *ever* happen to us. We're bulletproof now. If we survived the *Titanic*, we can survive anything, right, guys?"

"I never thought of it that way," David said, looking up.

"We need to pull ourselves together and figure out a strategy," Luke continued. "Let me think this through. People are going to ask us how we got here. We need to get our story straight."

"Maybe we should just tell them the truth," Isabel volunteered.

Isabel's natural inclination was always to tell the truth. Besides the fact that lying is just *wrong*, it also gets complicated. When you lie, then you have to remember the lie and who you told it to. It's a lot to remember.

"The truth?!" Julia looked at Isabel and shook her head. "Are you kidding? You want to tell people that we traveled through time and ended up on the deck of the *Titanic*? They'll put us in an insane asylum."

Julia sat back down on the bench.

"We have no birth certificates," Julia continued. "No paper trail. We have no proof that we existed before today."

"We already talked about this, remember?" David reminded the others. "We decided to pretend we were orphans. Our parents went down with the *Titanic*."

"Oh yeah! That's *good*," said Julia, who knew a good lie when she heard one. "That could work. I don't know if they kept careful records of who was on the ship."

"What's our money situation?" Luke asked Julia, who had been holding their cash.

She pulled out a wad of wet bills that John Jacob Astor—one of the wealthiest men in the world—had given to her before he perished on the *Titanic*.

"Eight hundred . . . nine hundred . . . a thousand bucks," Julia said after counting ten hundred-dollar bills.

That was a *lot* of money in 1912. The average salary in those days was $750 a year.

"That'll hold us for a while," Luke said. "But it won't last forever. We're gonna have to get jobs."

"Jobs?" David asked. "How are we gonna get jobs? We're kids."

"Kids had jobs in 1912," Isabel pointed out. "They didn't have child labor laws yet."

"I'm not going to work in some sweatshop for two dollars a week," Julia insisted.

"You won't have to work in a sweatshop," Luke assured her. "There are lots of other jobs we can get."

"Like what?" David asked. "Do you mind if I point out the obvious? I'm *black*. Do you think anybody's gonna hire *me* for a good job in 1912? Martin Luther King Jr. wasn't even born yet. Neither was Rosa Parks, Jackie Robinson, Malcolm X—"

"Look," Julia said, "*none* of us have to get jobs. Don't you guys remember? We talked about this. We've got something nobody else here has."

"What?" asked Isabel.

Julia lowered her voice to a whisper, as if anyone might be listening in to their conversation.

"We know what's going to *happen*," she said.

"When you go back in time, naturally you can predict the future."

David snapped his fingers and stood up excitedly.

"Luke, remember you told that Astor guy that the Red Sox were going to win the World Series?"

"Yeah, so?"

"Well, we could bet our thousand bucks on the Red Sox and make a bundle!"

"Brilliant. Just one problem," Luke told David. "The World Series isn't until October. It's April now. What are we gonna do for the next six months? We'll need to spend that money for food, a place to live, and other stuff."

"Oh yeah," David said, sitting back down on the bench.

Julia jumped off the bench again.

"No, you dopes!" she exclaimed. "You don't have to bet on the World Series to make money! I can't believe you all forgot. We talked about this, too. We can invent something that we have in our time but they don't have here! It will be brand-new to them. Remember?"

The Flashback Four had been through a lot over the last few days. It made sense for them to forget the idea they had discussed when they had been all stressed out and their lives were in danger. In fact, it made sense for them to block some of those memories out.

"The *zipper!*" shouted Luke, Isabel, and David.

Of course, the zipper. The modern zipper was perfected by a Swedish American engineer named Gideon Sundback in 1913. It took him four years to get a patent. If the Flashback Four could create a simple zipper in 1912 and sell it to a company that would manufacture it, they could make *millions*. It might not be fair to Gideon Sundback, but this was a matter of survival. And the kids would never have to work a day in their lives.

"How hard could it be?" Julia asked. "We just take some little pieces of metal, and—"

"I can do a schematic drawing," David volunteered. "My dad showed me how."

"That's a great idea!" Luke said. "Nobody will ever know we weren't the *real* inventors of the zipper."

"*I'll* know," Isabel said quietly. But she didn't make a big deal about it, because she couldn't think of a better way for the team to earn money.

By this time, the sun had set in the west over New Jersey, across the Hudson River. There was a chill in the air. The Flashback Four wrapped their clothes around themselves tightly.

"Well, we're not going to invent the zipper *tonight*," Luke told the others. "Right now, we'd better find a place to sleep."

A CRAZY IDEA

WHILE THE FLASHBACK FOUR WERE FIGURING OUT what to do next in 1912, there was a full-scale panic going on in the twenty-first-century office of Pasture Company (motto: "If I don't see you in the future, I'll see you in the pasture") in Boston, Massachusetts.

Miss Z picked up her phone and put it down again without dialing a number. Then she looked at her computer screen, and looked away from it.

"What are we going to do *now*?" she shouted to her assistant, Mrs. Ella Vader, gesturing wildly and nearly falling out of her wheelchair.

Miss Z suffered from ALS—amyotrophic lateral

sclerosis. It's a nervous-system disease that weakens muscles. There's no cure for it. But right now, ALS was not her biggest problem. No, Miss Z's biggest problem was the Flashback Four.

It was impossible to know if Luke, David, Julia, and Isabel were dead or alive. She didn't know what had happened to them at the moment she'd tried to whisk them back home from the deck of the *Titanic*. All she knew was that the kids had *not* arrived in her office, as expected.

Instead, she had inadvertently transported a *Titanic* deckhand named Thomas Maloney into the twenty-first century. Now he was sitting across from her, playing with the electric pencil sharpener on her desk. He was a big man, and he looked angry. Who could blame him?

"Mr. Maloney, tell me *exactly* what happened those last few moments on the *Titanic*," Miss Z asked.

"Like I told ya," he said, "I was at the front of the ship. It was tiltin' forward. The captain told me not to let anybody up there 'cause they might get swept off into the sea. Then these four kids show up and ask me to take a picture of 'em with some funny-lookin' camera. I told 'em to get out of there and get into a lifeboat, but they wouldn't budge. They offered me a thousand bucks to let 'em take the picture, so I say okay. And that's all I remember. Next thing I knew, I was here with you."

"And you have no idea what happened to the children?" asked Mrs. Vader.

"Nope."

"This is *bad*," said Miss Z.

While she fretted, Mr. Maloney looked around the office and the modern wonders it contained. He wasn't so impressed by Miss Z's computer or her time-traveling smartboard. It was the *little* things that astonished him. Thomas Maloney had never seen a fluorescent light, a Post-it Note, or wall-to-wall carpeting.

He stood up unsteadily and went over to the window. When he looked down at the streets of Boston, he grabbed hold of the windowsill for support. It was twenty-three floors up. He had never been so high. He had never even been inside an elevator.

A helicopter buzzed past the window, and Thomas Maloney looked at it with fear and wonder in his eyes.

"Holy hotcakes! What in the blazes was *that*?" he shouted.

But the wheels in his head were turning. He had recently read H. G. Wells's book *The Time Machine* and understood the concept of time travel. It had sunk into his brain that he had been transported over a hundred years into the future. And he was no dummy. There must be a way to turn this into money, he figured.

"So lemme get this straight," Mr. Maloney said. "You sent them kids back to my time with that doo-hickey, but instead of bringin' 'em back here again, you brought me instead. That right?"

"That's right," said Mrs. Vader. Miss Z was too upset to answer.

Thomas Maloney picked up a pencil off Miss Z's desk and stuck it in her electric pencil sharpener. He marveled as it whirred and put a point on the pencil in a few seconds. The only way he had ever sharpened a pencil before was with a knife, painstakingly shaving the wood away. He stuck the pencil back in the machine and sharpened it over and over again, watching it get smaller and smaller.

"Will you please *stop* that?" asked Mrs. Vader.

Miss Z was deep in thought. The Flashback Four were stuck in 1912, possibly for the rest of their lives. How would she tell their parents what had happened to them? There were four signed permission slips in her desk drawer. Within the hour, the parents would realize their children were missing. Then the phone calls would begin.

There would be lawsuits, for sure. *Multimillion-dollar* lawsuits. Miss Z had made a large fortune with Findamate, the online dating service she had created, but if the kids were gone, it would ruin her. She'd have nothing left, and her reputation would be shot.

Reputation? She realized that was the *least* of her worries. The police would get involved, of course. There would have to be a criminal investigation. How could she ever explain what had happened to these four kids? The cops would probably dig up her back-yard looking for the bodies. And they wouldn't find any.

She would go to jail, of course, and spend the rest of her life there. Everything she had ever accomplished would have been for nothing. She would always be remembered for the mysterious kidnapping of those four children, who were never heard from again.

And what was she going to do with this Maloney guy? He seemed like a real troublemaker.

Maloney was looking at the photos all over the walls, many of which had not been shot until long after his lifetime. He stared at the picture of Neil Armstrong on the moon and just shook his head.

This was not good. Miss Z's mind, usually so sharp, was scattered and confused.

Mrs. Vader was upset too. But she wasn't as personally invested in the Flashback Four, and so she was able to think more clearly.

"*Maybe* the kids were able to get on one of the lifeboats," she said hopefully. "What happened to the survivors of the *Titanic*?"

"A ship called the *Carpathia* picked them up," Miss Z said. "They were taken to New York City. So what?"

"Well, what if we used the Board to send Mr. Maloney to the spot where that ship docked in 1912?" suggested Mrs. Vader. "The kids should be there, right? Then couldn't we use the Board again to bring them back here? I know it's an outrageous idea, but is it possible?"

Miss Z wrinkled her brow and thought it over. Because of a technological glitch, the Board is unable to send the same people back to the same place or time more than once. But this was a *different* place and time, with different people. It wasn't out of the question. A little smile appeared at the corner of her mouth.

"That just might work!" she said excitedly. "What have we got to lose?"

"Let's try it!" said Mrs. Vader.

They snapped into action. Mrs. Vader turned

on the Board to warm it up. Then she took out her smartphone to look up the precise location where the *Carpathia* had docked in New York City. Miss Z rolled over to her computer and began tapping keys rapidly.

"Mr. Maloney, I would like you to stand in front of that large board over there, please," she told him.

Thomas Maloney didn't rush over to fulfill her request. He didn't get up from the chair.

"Wait one gosh-darned minute," he said, putting his feet up on the edge of Miss Z's desk. "Maybe I don't wanna go to New York. I kinda like it right here. Maybe I'll stick around awhile."

"You *can't* stick around," Miss Z said sternly. "You have to go back to your own time."

"Says who?"

Thomas Maloney leaned back in the chair and clasped his hands behind his head. He was feeling cocky. And wealthy. There were ten hundred-dollar bills in his pocket, a small fortune, to him. He wouldn't need to get a job for quite a while.

"America's still a free country, ain't it?" he asked. "The land of opportunity, right? Looks like you two are livin' the good life, with your fancy contraptions and such. I could get used to this."

Thomas Maloney was a big man, but Miss Z had sized him up and decided she could take him. She had negotiated hundreds of deals with politicians and businesspeople around the world. It shouldn't be that hard to cut a deal with a deckhand who'd never gone to high school.

"Mr. Maloney," she said. "Do you know how much it costs to rent an apartment here in Boston?"

Maloney thought it over. He had been paying twelve Irish pounds a month for a small flat in Belfast before setting sail on the *Titanic*.

"Oh, I don't know," he said. "Twenty pounds a month?"

Miss Z and Mrs. Vader laughed.

"Try two *thousand* American dollars," said Miss Z.

"You kiddin' me?"

That was about as much money as he earned all *year* working on ships. He calculated that the thousand dollars in his pocket would only pay for two weeks' worth of rent. No food.

Miss Z noticed that Thomas Maloney was wearing a wedding ring.

"And how much does it cost to take your wife out to dinner, may I ask?"

"About five pounds, give or take," he replied.

"It will cost you ten times that much money here," Miss Z told him. "Mr. Maloney, a gallon of gas costs over two dollars now. A gallon of milk is more than twice that."

Thomas Maloney was doing arithmetic in his head, quickly trying to convert American dollars into Irish pounds. He was starting to sweat.

"What's your wife's name, Mr. Maloney?" asked Mrs. Vader.

"Katie."

"I suppose you miss her."

Miss Z didn't say anything for a moment. She wanted to give Maloney time to form a mental image of his wife and realize he would never see her again. He may have had children, too.

"Think about it, Mr. Maloney," Miss Z finally told him. "You have no place to live here. No job. The thousand dollars in your pocket is not going to last long. And then there's your family . . ."

Family. There's something about that word. Everybody wants to go home to their family at some point.

Thomas Maloney looked out the window again. A jet plane flew by, startling him.

While he was thinking it over, Mrs. Vader had done

her research and found that the *Carpathia* had docked at Pier 54 in New York City, at the end of Fourteenth Street. If the Flashback Four had survived the *Titanic*, that's where they would be, at least for the time being. She wrote it out on a page of scrap paper for Miss Z.

"Okay, okay, I'll go back," Maloney finally agreed. "But I think I deserve some, uh, compensation for the trouble you put me through. I didn't ask for this mess. And it's gonna cost me a lot of dough to get back home to Ireland."

Miss Z sighed. She needed Maloney more than he needed her. Fortunately, she had more money than he could ever imagine. She was used to people asking her for cash. It's an occupational hazard of being extremely wealthy.

"Would another thousand be helpful?" she asked as she reached into her desk drawer for her checkbook.

Maloney had been hoping for a hundred. This was going to be a *big* payday.

"That'll do," he said quickly. "But in *bills*, please. You know as well as I do that I ain't gonna be able to cash your check in 1912."

"Smart thinking, Mr. Maloney," Miss Z said with a little smile.

She wheeled herself over to a safe on the wall behind one of her many pictures. She opened it and took out an envelope.

"You can count it if you want," she said as she handed it to him. "But I assure you there are a thousand dollars in here."

Maloney pocketed the envelope without opening it.

"It's been a pleasure doin' business with you," he said, getting up to stand in front of the Board.

"But you need to do something else for me," Miss Z said.

"What?"

"I'm going to send you to a specific location in New York City in the year 1912," Miss Z explained. "If those four children survived the sinking of the *Titanic*, that's where they will be. When you get there, I want you to gather them together at the exact spot where you landed so I can bring them back here. Do you understand?"

"What if they ain't there?" Maloney asked. "What if they went down with the ship?"

"That will be my problem," Miss Z said. "You keep my thousand dollars and continue on with your life. I promise you will never hear from me again."

"Sounds fair," Maloney said, "but I could really

use another thousand. . . ."

"Enough!" she shouted. "Our negotiation is complete. Quickly! Stand in front of the Board. They might have already left the pier. I just hope we're not too late."

Miss Z pointed a small remote control at the Board. It buzzed gently and flashed some quick messages to indicate it was booting up. She tapped the exact latitude and longitude of Pier 54 into the keyboard.

"Is this gonna hurt?" Thomas Maloney asked.

"You won't feel a thing," Mrs. Vader said. "Close your eyes for the next minute or so. There will be a very bright light. But it won't hurt."

The technology inside the Board is far too advanced for me or just about *anybody* to explain. Even if I could explain it, you would be bored to death and probably stop reading this book right now. So let me just say this. It *works*. You're going to have to trust me on this. You know how grown-ups always say you can accomplish anything if you put your mind to it? Well, imagine how much you can accomplish if you put your mind to something *and* throw in a few billion dollars for research and development.

The crucial point is that the Board can send a person—or a group of people—to any moment and any spot on the globe if it has the exact date, time, latitude, and longitude.

A buzzing sound came off the Board, and then it lit up in a brilliant blast of bright blue. It glowed for a few seconds, and then the blue split into five separate bands of different colors. Mr. Maloney peeked and caught a glimpse of the bands of color merging together to form one solid blast of intense white light. He closed his eyes again.

The light appeared to stretch out and away from the surface of the Board until it reached Mr. Maloney. The Board seemed to be sucking him into it.

"It will all be over in a matter of seconds," Miss Z said. "Hang on. Soon you will be back in the year 1912. Back to *your* time."

The Board began to hum and vibrate, a low-frequency rumbling that was pleasant to the ear. It was like the purring of a cat.

"This better work," Miss Z muttered under her breath.

Thomas Maloney began to flicker, as if a strobe light was shining on him. The humming was getting louder.

It was happening. Maloney was making the transition from one century to another. He had reached the point of no return.

"I could use . . . another hundred bucks," he said, trying to extend his hand.

"Good-bye, Mr. Maloney!"

And then he vanished.

ONE FOR ALL AND ALL FOR ONE

MEANWHILE, ON PIER 54 IN NEW YORK, THE FLASH-back Four were alone, depressed, and anxious about their future. And their past. It was getting dark and cold outside.

"We'd better find a place to sleep," Luke told the others as he stood up. "Let's go. It looks like that building down the street might be a hotel—"

All four of them stood up. At that instant, before anyone could take a step, there was a flash of bright light off to the right and a puff of smoke. And then, not more than ten feet away, Thomas Maloney appeared.

"Eeek!" screamed Isabel as she grabbed David's shirt.

David jumped back in terror, almost falling over and taking Luke down with him.

"Holy—"

Mr. Maloney stumbled for a moment before regaining his balance. Then he looked around to get his bearings.

"So we meet again," he said to the group.

"Who are *you*?" asked Julia.

"He's that guy!" said Luke, pointing. "The guy at our meeting spot on the *Titanic*! Remember? He disappeared from the deck just as I was about to take his picture. And now he's *here*!"

"Thomas Maloney at yer service," Mr. Maloney said, making a little bow before checking to see if he still had his envelope full of cash. "Nice to see we're all safe and sound on dry land."

"How did you get here?" asked David. "Where did you come from?"

"Boston, Massachusetts, from what I understand," he replied.

"Were you in a big office building?" asked Julia.

"That's right," Maloney replied. "Never seen one so

high. And there was an aeroplane flying around in the sky."

Luke snapped his fingers.

"Miss Z must have been trying to zap us back from the *Titanic*, but she zapped *him* back instead!" he said.

"You gotta be kidding me," said David.

"I couldn't believe it, neither," Mr. Maloney told them. "I met your lady friend. In the wheelchair. She gave me a thousand bucks to send you home."

"Hey, I gave you a thousand dollars so we could take your picture!" Julia said. "We never took it. By all rights you should give me that money back."

"By all rights *you* should be floatin' belly-up in the Atlantic," said Mr. Maloney. "And if it wasn't for me, you'd be stuck here forever. So you can kiss your thousand good-bye. Do you want to go back to your own time or not?"

"Of *course* we want to go back!" Isabel said.

"Then gather together in a group right over here," Maloney said. "That's what your lady friend told me to tell you. Hurry up. There ain't a lot of time."

Isabel, David, and Luke rushed to form a group, throwing their arms over each other's shoulders like football players in a huddle. Julia just stood without moving, as if she couldn't decide whether or not to join the group.

"What's the matter, Julia?" asked Isabel.

"Oh, I don't know," Julia replied. "I was thinking that I could do pretty well starting over again in 1912. Everything is a lot less expensive here."

"You *have* to come back with us!" Isabel shouted.

"Why?" Julia asked defensively. "If I stay here and live the rest of my life starting now, I'll know lots of stuff in advance that nobody else here knows. Think about it. I'll be able to predict who's going to win the presidential elections. I could make a fortune on the stock market because I'll know which companies, like McDonald's, are going to become huge. And if all else fails, I could invent the zipper."

"What's a zipper?" asked Thomas Maloney.

"See?" said Julia. "He has no idea what a zipper is!"

"Are you crazy?" Luke asked. "Forget about that zipper idea! This isn't a *game*. This is your life!"

"What about your parents?" asked Isabel. "Your friends? You're willing to give up the people you love just to make some money in 1912?"

Julia shrugged. She didn't have a great relationship with her parents, even though they had given her everything she ever desired. And to Julia, friends were disposable. She could always make new ones. She was good at that. And being pretty didn't hurt, no matter what century you live in.

The other three members of the Flashback Four held on to each other tightly.

"We'll miss you," Luke said. "Are you sure you don't want to come back home with us?"

"Think about it, Julia," Isabel told her. "It's 1912. They have no designer clothes in 1912. No malls. No credit cards . . ."

"I don't care about those things," Julia said.

"Horses pooped all over the street," Luke added. "Remember that."

"You better make up your mind fast," Mr. Maloney told Julia. "That wheelchair lady is gonna blast your friends outta here any second."

"No cell phones," added David.

Julia looked up.

"No cell phones?" she asked. "No selfies?"

"No Facebook, Twitter, or Instagram, either," David told her. "No social media."

"No internet," added Isabel.

"If you live to be a hundred years old," Luke told Julia, "you might make it to the year 2000. That's when the whole selfie thing started."

Julia thought about it for a moment, and then rushed over to join the rest of the Flashback Four.

"Okay, okay!" she said, throwing her arms around their shoulders. "I'm in."

"One for all and all for one!" hollered Luke.

"Oh, one last thing before you go," said Mr. Maloney. "For everything you put me through, I should get some extra compensation, don't you think?"

"Compensation? What's that?" asked Isabel.

"He wants to be paid *again*," Luke explained.

"Forget it!" Julia yelled. "That's extortion! I already gave you a thousand dollars, for nothing!"

At that moment, a crackling sound filled the air. Isabel, Luke, David, and Julia stopped moving, as if they had been gripped by a powerful invisible force.

"What's happening?" asked Isabel.

"She's bringing us back," Julia whispered.

Indeed, she was.

Like I said, it's a complicated process, so I'm not going to bore you with the technological details. Suffice it to say, Miss Z activated the Board. Five multi-color bands flashed on it. They merged into one bright white light, and a few seconds later the Board began to pull the Flashback Four in, atom by atom. Molecule by molecule. The kids were flickering in the air now. They were being digitally uploaded from one century to the next.

Just as they were about to disappear, Luke called out to Mr. Maloney. "Oh, by the way," he said. "Have fun trying to spend any of that twenty-first-century money here in 1912. It hasn't been printed yet. They'll just think it's counterfeit."

"Hey! What the—" Maloney shouted.

"So long, sucker!" yelled David.

And then they vanished.

THE END OF THE FLASHBACK FOUR

IN BOSTON, MISS Z STARED AT THE BOARD intently. There were so many things that could go wrong with the technology, not to mention the human factor. And Thomas Maloney was a wild card. There was nothing to stop him from just taking the money and running as soon as he arrived back in 1912.

"This better work," Mrs. Vader said quietly.

"If it doesn't, my life is over," said Miss Z, her sweaty hands clutching the armrests of her wheelchair.

The screen suddenly lit up. Within a few seconds the bands of color fused together into one hot, white light.

"I think it's happening!" Mrs. Vader said excitedly.

"Let's hope we didn't scoop up that Maloney guy again," said Miss Z. "Or some total stranger."

The light crackled and jumped off the Board a few feet like tiny bolts of lightning. A humming sound filled the room, and a coffee cup vibrated on Miss Z's desk.

"Here we come!" shouted the voice of Isabel, holding hands tightly with David and Julia.

The Board was flashing like a strobe light, with bits and pieces of the Flashback Four appearing in two centuries at the same time. Miss Z and Mrs. Vader shielded their eyes.

And then, in an explosion of light, Luke, Isabel, Julia, and David appeared in the flesh a few feet in front of the Board. They fell into the room, coughing and stumbling, grabbing on to each other for support. Luke got down on the floor and kissed it, then jumped back up to hug his friends.

"We're back, baby!" David said. "I never thought I'd live to see this place again."

Across the room, Miss Z and Mrs. Vader were tearfully hugging each other, nearly collapsing with relief.

To the Flashback Four, Miss Z seemed older than she had been just a few days earlier. She looked grayer, more haggard. The sparkle that had been in her eyes seemed to be gone. She hadn't slept in several days.

Hesitantly, the kids approached her. They had returned without the nice clothes she had bought for them to wear on the *Titanic*. More importantly, they had returned without the TTT, the device that allowed them to text through time with her. Miss Z had invested a good part of her fortune to build it.

As a group, they were prepared for her to be angry. She had fired them after the Gettysburg mission, and she had every right to fire them again.

"We're *so* sorry," Isabel said. "We lost the TTT. That's why you lost contact with us."

"It got swept off the deck of the *Titanic*," David added. "We tried to grab it, but it was gone."

"I know you spent a lot of money on it," Julia said. "We'll pay you back, little by little. I promise. I'll give you my babysitting money for the rest of my life."

"Shhh, don't be silly," said Miss Z, a finger to her lips. "The TTT is just a bunch of circuits and silicon. It's replaceable. We're just so glad you're back." Then she reached out her arms for each of the Flashback Four to hug her.

This took the kids by surprise. Up until this point,

Miss Z had not showed them a lot of warmth or compassion. She seemed quite serious and businesslike. But now, she was slobbering like a baby.

"Are we fired?" Isabel asked timidly.

"Goodness, no!" Miss Z replied. "Whatever happened out there was my fault. I made a big mistake. I never should have sent you on such a dangerous mission. I can't imagine what I was thinking."

"Don't blame yourself," David said.

"I do," Miss Z continued. "My big mistake was choosing a meeting spot at the front of the *Titanic*. That was the first part of the ship to go underwater! I should have *known* that was going to happen. I wasn't thinking. Now I'm kicking myself. If you kids had been stuck in 1912, I never would have forgiven myself. That's why I've decided to discontinue the Flashback Four program."

"What?!"

After everything that happened on the *Titanic*, none of the kids had any intention of traveling through time again. But even so, it was upsetting to hear that the whole program was going to be scrapped.

"My plan was to send you on another mission after you came back from this one," Miss Z told them.

"But I've been thinking about this a lot over the last couple of days. I can't have you risk your lives again. We dodged bullets on the first two missions. Traveling through time is simply too dangerous. I thank you for everything you've done up until this point. I'm sorry it had to end this way, but I'm so grateful you're back and safe. You kids had better go home now. I'm sure your parents are worried sick about you."

Mrs. Vader opened the door, in case the kids didn't get the hint that it was time for them to leave.

"But what about the museum you were planning to build?" David asked.

Miss Z had made her fortune by creating a dating service that brought millions of lonely people together. But that's not how she wanted to be remembered after she was gone. She wanted to create a museum that would show the world photos of great events in history—especially events that had never been photographed before.

Miss Z sighed.

"It wasn't meant to be," she replied. "Look, I'm tired. My condition is worsening, and the stress of this *Titanic* incident didn't help any. I've got to face reality. I'm running out of time. Most people in my condition only last a few years. I've been lucky. I think I should just retire, maybe do some traveling, and enjoy whatever time I have left. I probably wouldn't have lived to see my museum completed anyway."

"But it was so important to you," said Isabel, looking around the office at the photographs on the walls.

"You're right. It was," replied Miss Z. "But I cannot in good conscience put you young people in the position of risking your lives just so I can have some photos. I'm not willing to play with people's lives that way."

"It wasn't just so *you* could have the photos," David said. "It's so the *world* could have the photos."

"I'm sorry," said Miss Z. "My mind is made up."

The Flashback Four got up and moved toward the door. It was at that point that Luke stopped and turned around.

"That reminds me," he said to Miss Z. "We have something to show you."

Luke took the little camera out of his pocket and turned it on. The battery was almost out of juice, but there was just enough to last a few minutes. Luke found the picture he'd taken of the *Titanic* and held it up for Miss Z to see.

She gasped.

"Oh my," Miss Z said, her eyes getting moist with tears. "You actually got the picture?"

"You told us to get the shot," Luke replied. "So we got it."

Miss Z stared at the photo for a long time. She picked up a magnifying glass from her desk drawer to examine it more closely.

"So *this* is what it looked like when the *Titanic* was about to go down," she said, holding the camera carefully. "It is marvelous! And it's the only photo like it in the world. How did you do it?"

The Flashback Four gathered around her once again.

"After that Maloney guy disappeared from the front of the ship, we figured we would never get back here," Luke told her. "So we tried to get into a lifeboat, but they were either filled up or they had already been launched half empty."

"So we jumped off the *Titanic* into the water," Julia said. "It was *so* cold."

"They taught me how to swim," said David. The others laughed, remembering.

"We managed to get over to a lifeboat," Luke continued. "That's where I took this shot. A few minutes after I pushed the button, the *Titanic* was gone."

"It was amazing!" said Isabel.

Miss Z looked at the Flashback Four with wonder and admiration.

"I wish I had been there," she said. "Well, I mean, I wish I could have seen it with my own eyes. But this is certainly the next best thing. You've done the world a remarkable service. You captured a piece of history that would have been lost forever."

Miss Z stared at the photo some more. The sparkle was back in her eyes.

IT'S ALL DOWNHILL FROM HERE

TO THE READER: BEFORE WE CONTINUE WITH THE story, a word of warning. This chapter includes quite a bit of information about volcanoes. Now, if you think reading about volcanoes could possibly be boring, feel free to skip ahead and flip to the end of this chapter, when things get exciting again for the Flashback Four. But you'll be missing out, because volcanoes are *very* cool. So you may want to stick around and read the whole chapter.

Unless, of course, you're in a big hurry to get somewhere. But if you're in such a hurry to get somewhere, what are you doing reading this book in the first place? You should be at that other place doing that more important thing.

In any case, after getting back to Boston, Luke, Isabel, Julia, and David went home. They went back to their regular lives of school, sports, church, family, and so on. Their time-traveling career was over. Life returned to normal. None of the kids told their parents or friends about what they had experienced. What would have been the point? Nobody would ever believe it.

But something was different about them, and they could all feel it. The four of them shared a secret—they were *survivors*. They had survived the adventure in Gettysburg, where they had been physically attacked and thrown in jail. They had survived the sinking of the *Titanic*, where they had jumped off the ship and nearly drowned. Living through a traumatic event changes a person, and it bonds groups of survivors together.

A few weeks later, Isabel was walking to science class. She was a good student who liked school, except that she had to put up with some of the immature boys in her grade, who tended to be obnoxious and not take their studies seriously.

When Isabel showed up for science class, there was a sign on the door. . . .

TODAY'S CLASS MEETS IN THE COURTYARD

When she got outside, the science teacher, Mr. Martin, was in the middle of the courtyard wearing a dirty apron, work boots, and protective goggles.

"Nice getup, Mr. M," one of the boys commented. "You going to a wedding or something today?"

"No," the teacher replied. "We're going to make a volcano."

"Cool!" everyone exclaimed.

Mr. Martin was one of the few teachers in the school who hadn't given up on doing innovative, interesting projects to try to keep the students—and especially the boys—engaged.

"Can anybody tell me what a volcano is?" he asked when everyone in the class had arrived.

Stuart, probably the most obnoxious of the obnoxious boys, didn't bother waiting to be called on.

"It's like when the wind starts whipping around and it picks up Dorothy's house and stuff," he announced to the class. "And then, *bam*, the house lands in Munchkinland."

"That's a tornado, you dope!" said one of the other boys.

"Actually," Mr. Martin said, "the word *volcano* comes from the Roman god of fire, Vulcan."

"Like on *Star Trek*, right?" asked Stuart. "Wasn't Dr. Spock a Vulcan?"

"I think you mean *Mr.* Spock," Mr. Martin said wearily as he bent down to pick up a clump of dirt. "Dr. Spock was a pediatrician. But we're getting off topic. I'm talking about volcanoes here. You see, the Earth's crust is broken into seventeen tectonic plates that fit together like a giant jigsaw puzzle. They move and float on a soft mantle below the surface of the Earth."

"*Mickey* Mantle is below the surface of the Earth too," shouted Stuart. "Ever since he dropped dead!"

Proud of his little joke, Stuart turned around to collect high fives from his friends. Mr. Martin waited for their cackling to subside before continuing.

Julia rolled her eyes. It was hard for her to believe that a boy like Stuart might one day grow up to become a productive member of society. None of the girls had said a word. They were just standing around, sneaking peeks at their cell phones.

"Mantle is liquid rock," said Mr. Martin. "Sometimes the tectonic plates push and grind against each other to form a mountain." He brought over a big red plastic garbage can while the boys elbowed each other and giggled because the teacher had used the word *grind*.

While the boys cracked wise, Isabel pulled a pad from her backpack and began taking notes. There might be a test on this material. And even if there wasn't a test, she reasoned, this was information that could be useful to know down the line. *You never know when it might come in handy,* she thought.

"And sometimes the molten rock—or magma—from the Earth's upper mantle works its way to the surface," Mr. Martin continued. "When the pressure from the gases within the molten rock gets too great, it erupts."

"Can we blow something up now?" asked Stuart. "That's the cool part."

"Yeah, explosions are awesome," said one of the other boys.

"We'll get to the explosion in a minute," said Mr. Martin. "Patience is a virtue that you boys would be wise to cultivate."

He turned on a spigot on the courtyard wall and used a garden hose to fill the garbage can with water. When the level was about three-quarters of the way up to the top, he added a cup of red food coloring to the water.

"Hey, Mr. Martin," said one of the boys. "Since when

does a volcano look like a garbage can? We made a volcano out of papier-mâché when I was in third grade, and it didn't look nothing like that."

"It didn't look *anything* like that," Mr. Martin said, unable to restrain himself from correcting the boy's grammar. "There are different kinds of volcanoes. This one is going to be an *explosive* volcano. So we need to add millions of tons of boulders and volcanic debris."

He opened a plastic bag full of ping-pong balls and dumped them into the water.

Next, Mr. Martin took an empty plastic soda bottle and attached a brick to either side of it using duct tape.

"What's that for, Mr. Martin?" somebody asked.

"You'll see," the teacher replied. "When molten rock pours out of a volcano, it's called lava. It's really hot, but it moves slowly, so people can usually evacuate in time. Sometimes though, the top of the mountain will just *explode* and release millions of tons of ash, flying boulders, pulverized rock, and poisonous gases."

"I think there was one of those volcanoes in the boys' bathroom yesterday," Stuart cracked. "Whew! Talk about poisonous gases! We all had to evacuate."

"WILL YOU SHUT UP FOR ONCE IN YOUR LIFE?" Isabel suddenly shouted. "Do you have to be stupid *all* the time?"

Her outburst even shocked herself. She was usually quiet in school. Most of the time, she limited her displays of disgust to eye rolling and head shaking. But after everything she had been through on the *Titanic* and at Gettysburg, Isabel had lost some of her timidity and gained some confidence to say what was on her mind.

Everybody stopped for a moment and looked at her. Even Stuart was shocked. He had no comeback. A few of the girls clapped their hands quietly.

"Anyway," said Mr. Martin, "when the top of the mountain explodes, the result is called pyroclastic flow. It moves at the speed of a hurricane and can get as hot as eighteen *hundred* degrees."

Mr. Martin put the bottle gently on the ground. Then he stuck a funnel in it and began to fill it. Kids began covering their ears.

"What's that stuff, Mr. Martin?" somebody asked.

"Liquid nitrogen," the teacher replied. "You can also use ammonium dichromate."

He quickly capped the soda bottle and lowered it into the garbage can full of water.

"Now stand back, everybody!" he announced. "It should be about ten seconds."

The class began counting down.

"Ten . . . nine . . . eight . . . seven . . . six . . . five . . . four . . . three . . . two . . . one!"

Nothing happened.

A few more seconds passed. A little smoke started rising out of the garbage can. And then, *BOOM*!

The soda bottle blew its top, and red water, smoke, and ping-pong balls were launched in the air and rained down all over the courtyard.

"Whoa!" "Cool!" "Awesome!"

"That's what you call a Plinian eruption," Mr. Martin announced. "Of course, if this had been a *real* volcano, it would be no laughing matter. There would be death and destruction for the people who live in the area. There could be earthquakes, landslides, acid rain, or flash floods."

Mr. Martin had a satisfied grin as he looked at the students' faces. Even Stuart and his obnoxious pals were locked in now. It's just about impossible to be bored when you're watching an explosion. Blowing stuff up is undeniably cool.

"The biggest known volcano in our solar system is on Mars," Mr. Martin told the class. "It's three hundred seventy-three miles wide and thirteen miles high."

Nobody said "whoa" or "cool" or "awesome."

Mr. Martin went on to tell the students about some

other famous volcanoes, but almost immediately, he realized he had pushed his luck. Isabel was still jotting down notes, but most of the class had already lost interest and were chatting about other things.

Mr. Martin sighed, silently lamenting the short attention span of today's kids. Maybe they got *something* out of the demonstration, he hoped.

A few minutes after the dismissal bell rang, Isabel was at her locker. She turned on her cell phone to find a group text already in progress. . . .

Julia: What R you guys doing?

Luke: ZIP. U?

David: Want 2 get pizza?

Julia: Where?

Luke: I'M IN. WHERE ISABEL?

David: Meet at Boylston and Tremont in 30

Boylston Street and Tremont Street intersect at the corner of Boston Common, one of the prettiest parks in America. The Boston subway, which is called the T, stops right nearby, so it was a convenient meeting spot for the Flashback Four.

The group hadn't seen each other since getting back from their *Titanic* adventure, so a long group hug was in order. Then they grabbed slices at a nearby pizza joint and sat down on a bench on the south side of the park. It reminded them of the bench they'd ended up on when the *Carpathia* had docked in New York.

"It feels weird, doesn't it?" David asked after the usual pleasantries had been covered.

"Yeah," Julia replied. "What is it?"

"I don't know," said Isabel. "I've just been feeling strange ever since we got back. It's like I'm a different person or something."

"Me too," David said. "Can't put my finger on it."

"I can," Luke said. "I'm bored. We're all bored. We were on the *Titanic*. We almost *died*. Now we're back home, going to boring school. Doing boring home-work. Living boring lives."

"It *was* exciting, wasn't it?" Isabel said a little mis-chievously. "I still can't believe we made it back."

"That will probably be the most exciting thing that ever happens to any of us," Julia noted. "It's a little depressing, huh?"

"Remember when that rich guy—John Jacob Astor—gave us his money?" recalled Isabel.

"Remember when he locked us in that stateroom, and then the ship hit the iceberg?" recalled Luke.

"That was cool," David said. "I mean, it wasn't cool

at the time, but it's cool to think about now that it's over."

"Face it," Luke told the others. "We're officially boring now. We'll never do anything that exciting again. It's all downhill from here."

They walked through Boston Common in silence until they reached the famous Frog Pond near the north end of the park. Some kids were tossing a Frisbee back and forth. A couple was taking selfies on the bridge in front of the famous swan boats. That's when Luke noticed a couple of women across the pond. One of them was sitting in a wheelchair.

"Wait a minute," he said. "Is that . . ."

"Miss Z!" Isabel shouted.

The foursome ran over find Miss Z with Mrs. Vader sitting near the edge of the pond, tossing pieces of bread into the water for the ducks. The office of Pasture Company in the John Hancock Tower was just a few blocks away.

More hugs were dispensed, and the two women greeted the kids warmly.

"It's so good to see you!" Mrs. Vader said.

"We framed that wonderful photo you took of the *Titanic* as it was sinking," Miss Z told the kids, "and we hung it in the empty space on the wall."

"What are you doing out here?" asked Isabel.

"I guess I'm . . . semi-retired," Miss Z replied, tossing the last of her bread into the water. "Living the good life, as they say. It's a little dull, if the truth be known. What are *you* kids doing out here? School must be over for the day."

"We were a little bored too," said Julia.

"Bored?" Miss Z looked surprised. "How can you possibly be bored? What are you in, sixth grade? You have your whole lives ahead of you!"

"Yes, shouldn't you be home playing video games or something?" asked Mrs. Vader. "Isn't that what your generation does for fun?"

"Oh, I don't know," Luke replied. "Video games just aren't the same anymore. They're not like jumping off the *Titanic*."

"I guess not," Miss Z said. "Simulating reality is not quite the same thing as experiencing it."

The Flashback Four helped wheel Miss Z back to her office in the Hancock building. Always the good hostess, Mrs. Vader offered the kids some cookies before they left. The Flashback Four, of course, accepted.

"You said you were planning to send us on another

mission after we got back from the *Titanic*," Julia asked. "What was it?"

Miss Z hesitated, then glanced at Mrs. Vader. "It doesn't matter anymore," she said. "I'm retired. The program is over."

"Please?" the Flashback Four begged.

"Well, I guess there's no harm in just *talking* about it," said Miss Z. "What do you kids think of when I say the word *Pompeii*?"

HOLD ON TIGHT

POMPEII.

It's pronounced *pom-PAY.* To some people, the word means nothing. To others, it's the greatest tragedy in human history.

"That's the name of some old movie, right?" asked David.

"Isn't pompeii some weird hairdo from the 1950s?" asked Luke.

"That's pompadour, you dope," Julia told him.

"I learned about Pompeii at school today," Isabel told the group. "It was a city in the Roman Empire. There was a volcano nearby, and it erupted. The whole city was buried in ash and disappeared. They didn't find it for over a thousand years."

"Very *good*, Isabel," said Miss Z. "Would one of you mind getting that globe near the window?"

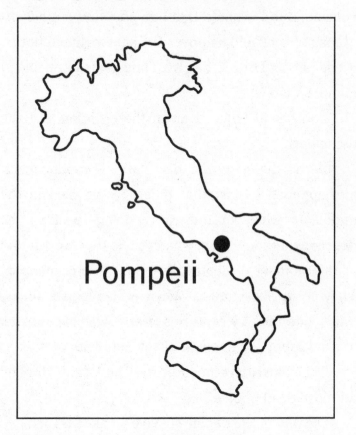

David went to get the globe. Miss Z lowered her voice almost to a whisper. "Here's the story. It was August twenty-fourth in the year 79 AD. Pompeii was on the western shore of Italy, next to the Bay of Naples.

Right *here*. It wasn't called Italy back then. About ten miles away was Mount Vesuvius, a volcano that had been dormant since 920 BC. If the people of Pompeii knew it was a volcano at all, they figured it was a dead volcano. But it erupted that day, shooting out *billions* of tons of rock and ash over the next eighteen hours. It completely buried the city. Thousands of people in Pompeii died."

"Cool," said Luke. "I mean the eruption, not the dying part."

"Here's the *interesting* part," Miss Z continued. "It all happened so fast that those people died in the middle of whatever they were doing—walking the dog, cooking some food, whatever. So they were found at the moment of death, preserved in volcanic ash. They were like statues. When archeologists finally unearthed the city centuries later, it was like looking at a snapshot of a moment of ancient history."

"That must have been gross," Julia said, "finding all those dead bodies."

"Did any of the people survive?" asked Isabel.

"Yes, some people got out fast and escaped," replied Miss Z. "But for the people who stayed, their whole city was wiped out."

"And you were going to send us *there*?" asked

David, incredulous. "That would be even more dangerous than putting us on the *Titanic*. At least on the *Titanic* we had the chance to be rescued."

"Well, my plan was to send you to Pompeii to take a picture of Mount Vesuvius as it was erupting," Miss Z told them. "You see, it took about a half an hour before all that stuff fell from the sky and landed on the city. In that half hour I would have gotten you out of there safely. That was my thinking, anyway."

"I don't get it," Julia said. "Why didn't the people get out of Pompeii as soon as the volcano erupted? Why didn't they evacuate the whole city?"

"Many people tried to get out," Miss Z explained. "It wasn't so easy."

"Yeah, it's not like they could catch a plane or a train out of town," Isabel said. "It was the year 79."

"Right," Miss Z said, "and a lot of people just decided to stay put in their houses, waiting for the eruption to blow over."

"Wait a minute," Luke interrupted. "How do we know any of this stuff is true? They didn't have radio, TV, or internet in those days. Was paper even invented?"

"Oh yes, they had paper," Miss Z replied. "We know what happened in Pompeii mainly because a teenager named Pliny the Younger watched the eruption from his uncle's home across the Bay of Naples. He wrote down everything that happened."

"That eruption would have made a cool picture for your museum," said Isabel.

"Yes," Miss Z said wistfully. "For a long time I've been fantasizing about getting a photo for my collection of an event that took place before photography was invented. The first photograph was taken in the 1820s. So we really don't know for sure what the world looked like before that time. Imagine this—a picture of Mount Vesuvius erupting in the year 79. Talk about a snapshot of a moment of ancient history! How cool would that be?"

"Cool," said Isabel.

"Way cool," said Julia.

"Moderately cool," said David.

"I've always wanted to go to Italy," said Luke, whose father was half Italian. "They have the best pizza in the world there, you know. Pizza was invented in Italy."

"I love pizza," David replied.

"*Everybody* loves pizza," added Isabel.

"I heard pizza was invented in China," Julia said.

"Get outta here!" Luke said. "Whoever heard of Chinese pizza?"

"Lots of stuff was invented in China," said Isabel,

who had written a report on the subject in fourth grade. "Gunpowder, paper, the compass, printing . . ."

"Did they have pizza in ancient Pompeii?" asked Luke, who was clearly obsessed with pizza.

"I don't know if they had it in the year 79," Miss Z replied with a laugh. "But I bet you can get it there now."

"Now?" asked David. "You mean Pompeii is a city again?"

"Yes, and a big tourist attraction," said Miss Z. "Millions of people go there every year. In fact, after I finished college, I took a trip to Italy and visited Pompeii. It was *amazing*."

"I went there too," added Mrs. Vader. "It's one of those places everybody should go in their lifetime."

"I wish I could go," said Isabel.

"Hey, couldn't you use the Board to send us to Pompeii right *now*?" Luke asked Miss Z. "I mean, not ancient Pompeii. Couldn't you send us to Pompeii in the present day? You can type in any year you want, right? So you could type in *this* year."

"Yeah, you could beam us over there instantly," David said.

"That's not a bad idea," said Julia.

"Oh, I don't think so," Miss Z told them. "Not after

what you've been through."

"Let's do it!" Luke said excitedly. "Just for a few minutes? We don't have to take any pictures or anything. We can just go, look around, and come right back. Nothing would go wrong."

"What about *this* idea?" suggested Miss Z. "Perhaps I could send you kids to Pompeii with your families. All expenses paid. It would be a little present from me to make up for everything I've put you through."

"No thanks," said Julia. "I don't want to go away with my family."

"I haven't gone on vacation with my family since I was eight," said Luke.

"Yeah, I'm too old to go on vacation with my parents," David said.

Isabel kept her mouth shut. She had gone on vacation to the Dominican Republic with her parents over Christmas vacation.

"We want to go to Pompeii with *you*," Luke told Miss Z. "You can be our chaperone. That way, when we do something stupid, you'll be able to bail us out."

"You *did* say you wanted to travel now that you're retired," added Isabel.

"I think it's a marvelous idea!" said Mrs. Vader, clapping her hands together. "I can stay here at the office to send all five of you to Pompeii and bring you back."

"It *would* be interesting to visit Pompeii again," Miss Z admitted.

"Please please please please please?" begged the kids.

"Well . . . okay," Miss Z said. "But it will have to be fast. Just one hour and back."

"Yay!"

"Wait a minute," Isabel said. "We can't go. We lost the TTT on the *Titanic*."

Miss Z opened her desk drawer. There was a TTT in it.

"This is the last one I have," she said, handing it to Isabel.

"I'm going to type in the Porta Marina gate at Pompeii as our meeting spot," said Miss Z. "One hour should be enough to give us a quick taste of the city. Mrs. Vader, will you kindly zap us back here exactly one hour from now?"

"Will do," Mrs. Vader replied, checking her watch.

Isabel grabbed her backpack and put the TTT into one of the zippered pockets.

"No way I'm going to lose it *this* time," she said.

Luke, Isabel, Julia, and David rolled Miss Z over

to the Board and crowded around her to form a tight group.

"Okay, is everybody ready?" asked Mrs. Vader, typing some commands on the keyboard.

"Ready as we'll ever be," replied Miss Z. "This is exciting!"

The Board began to buzz and glow bright blue for a few seconds. Then the light split into five color bands that merged into a solid band of bright white light.

"Hold on tight, everybody," said Mrs. Vader.

The Board began to hum and vibrate as the light reached out to envelop the group.

"It's happening!" Miss Z exclaimed.

The group began to flicker. The humming got louder.

And the next thing anyone knew, the Flashback Four and Miss Z had disappeared.

BACK TO THE PRESENT

WHEN MISS Z OPENED HER EYES AND SAW THAT she had been transported from Boston to Pompeii in the snap of a finger, a smile spread across her face. It made her look twenty years younger.

"It *works*!" she marveled. "I mean, I knew it would work. But I never thought I would actually *see* it work."

Pompeii was a fortress city, built to repel an enemy invasion. It was—and still is—surrounded by a double wall, with seven gates. The Flashback Four (along with Miss Z and her wheelchair) landed about ten feet outside the Porta Marina gate, the main entry point. From there, they could see the ruins of the ancient city spread out in front of them, stretching into the distance.

"Are you okay?" David asked Miss Z, bending over her wheelchair.

"It's just like I remember it," she replied.

Isabel pulled the TTT out of her backpack and composed a short text to Mrs. Vader. . . .

WE R HERE

The TTT, having only to transmit text across distance and not across time, flashed a response almost right away. . . .

HAVE FUN! SEE YOU IN AN HOUR.

More than a million tourists visit Pompeii every year, so naturally it's somewhat of a tourist trap. Right outside the Porta Marina gate were some small shops that sold snacks, guidebooks, postcards, refrigerator magnets, and other trinkets.

Some young men immediately surrounded the group with cries of "*Buongiorno!* Do you speak English?" They were offering to sell fruit, coral jewelry, and bottles of water. Professional guides offered to give the kids a tour. Beggars who spoke no English held out their hands and silently asked for money.

There were signs all over the shops. Some of the

words were written in Italian, but many were written in English for the sake of American tourists. Like *PIZZA*.

"Pizza!" shouted the Flashback Four.

"Can we get some pizza?" asked Julia.

The other three looked at Miss Z with their puppy-dog eyes.

"Well . . . okay."

"Yay!"

Miss Z bought a margherita pizza (named after Margherita, the queen of Italy) and the kids quickly devoured it. It wasn't the best pizza in the world, but it was special because it came from the place where pizza was invented.

"This is *real* Italian pizza," Luke announced. "From Italy."

Tickets to enter the ruins cost thirteen euros per person. Miss Z paid with her credit card.

"Be careful," she advised as she handed a ticket to each of the kids. "Anyplace there are a lot of tourists, there will be pickpockets."

"What if we get robbed?" asked Isabel.

"We're not going to get robbed," David assured her.

"I know karate," said Luke. "Stick with me."

"This will be our meeting spot," Miss Z told the kids. "Let's stay together as a group. But if we should be separated for any reason, we'll meet right back here in a little less than one hour, at one o'clock. Got it?"

"One hour, one o'clock," replied David.

"Now, before we enter the city, turn around and look behind you."

The Flashback Four turned around. There it was, about ten miles to the north, looming over the city—Vesuvius. It's a huge blue-gray mountain with two peaks, over four thousand feet high and stretching about eight miles across. If modern Italy is the shape of a boot, Mount Vesuvius is toward the top front edge of the boot.

"Is that Mount Vesuvius?" asked Isabel. Miss Z nodded her head.

"It's still there!" marveled Julia.

"Well, of course it's still there," David said, rolling his eyes. "Where's it going to go? It's a *mountain.*"

"But it was a taller mountain before it blew its top," said Miss Z. "Almost twice as high."

"How do we know it won't erupt again?" asked Isabel, a little nervously.

"We don't."

It was the truth. Vesuvius is still an active volcano. It has erupted *eighty* times since the big one in the year 79. The most recent eruption was in 1944.

The group entered the gate. Luke pushed Miss Z's wheelchair with David's assistance, and it wasn't easy. The street was unpaved. It was made of large, flat stones that fit together like a jigsaw puzzle.

The town is surprisingly large, about a mile from end to end. It had been laid out in a grid, like a modern

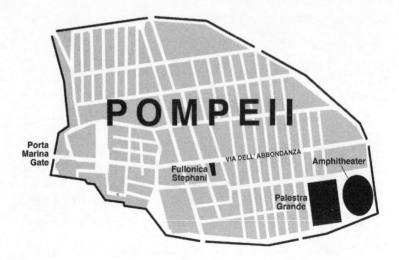

city. The group set off down the main street, which is called Via dell'Abbondanza.

"There was no country named Italy in the year 79," Miss Z told the kids, like a tour guide. "Pompeii was part of the Roman Empire, which ruled over southern Europe along the Mediterranean Sea for five hundred years."

Walking through Pompeii felt like going back in time (that is, if you ignored the tour groups and cell phones). Via dell'Abbondanza was lined with stone and brick ruins of houses, shops of all kinds, and even restaurants. The ancient Romans liked going out to eat. There were twenty bakeries in town when the volcano erupted. In one of them, eighty-one loaves of bread were found in an oven.

The kids noticed the sidewalks were higher than the ones back home. This is because the streets were flooded with water every night to flush away dirt and waste. The Romans were masters at moving water from one place to another. They built aqueducts to carry water from rivers and lakes that were *miles* from the city, using only gravity to do the work.

It's hard to believe, but houses in Pompeii had running water. Twenty-five fountains were scattered at intersections around the town. There were public baths that had pools of hot, warm, and cold water to soak in. This took amazing technology, considering the fact that they didn't have pumps, steel, plastics, cranes, bulldozers, electricity, trucks, or computers in the year 79.

Julia noticed that many of the buildings had a jug on the ground outside the doorway. She asked Miss Z about them.

"People would leave their pee in those jugs to be taken away," she explained.

"Where did they take it?" Julia asked. "What did they do with it?"

"Do you really want to know?" asked Miss Z.

"No," Julia replied. "I'm sure it's gross."

"Where did kids go to school?" asked Isabel.

"They haven't dug up any schools or classrooms," Miss Z told her. "Teachers would just take their students out in the street or anywhere it was convenient for a lesson."

Isabel took the TTT out of her backpack again and sent a quick text to Mrs. Vader. . . .

HAVING FUN. WISH YOU WERE HERE.

SO DO I was the quick reply.

Miss Z told Luke to stop pushing her wheelchair for a moment.

"Think of it," she told them. "*All* of this, the entire city, was covered by twenty feet of ash after Vesuvius erupted. It formed a seal around the city. That's why these ruins are still here today for us to see."

"So it's sort of like a big time capsule," Isabel noted.

"Yes!" Miss Z agreed. "Isn't it ironic? The volcano completely destroyed Pompeii, but at the same time it preserved Pompeii."

She told the kids how the city had sat undisturbed under that layer of ash for over fifteen hundred years. And then, in 1748, it was rediscovered. Ever since then, archeologists have been uncovering this lost city, piece by piece. To this day, there are still parts of Pompeii that haven't been excavated.

"It's like a ghost town," Miss Z said. "But the ghosts

are still here. Let me show you something."

A little farther down the street was a small glass building, like a greenhouse. When the group got closer, they could see it was filled with white figures of men, women, children, and animals posed in different positions. They looked almost like sculptures.

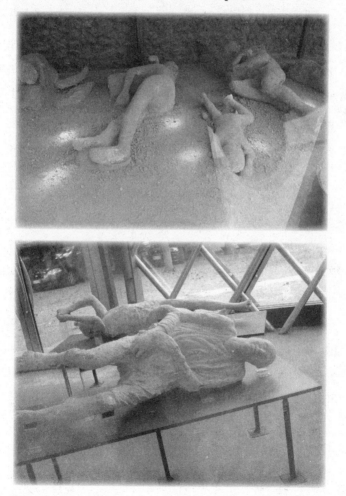

"Are they mummies?" David asked.

"No," Miss Z said. "They're not even dead bodies."

She explained that over the centuries, the bodies of the victims had disintegrated under all that volcanic ash. That left cavities in the shapes of their bodies. In 1860, a very clever archeologist named Giuseppe Fiorelli came up with the idea of drilling small holes into the ash and pouring liquid plaster into the cavities. After the plaster hardened, he chipped away the ash to discover the shapes of bodies at the moment they died. Hundreds of figures were unearthed this way.

"That's creepy," Isabel said, looking away.

"I think it's cool," said Julia.

"Fortunately, these people didn't suffer for long," said Miss Z. "Maybe a few seconds. It must have been like swallowing fire."

The Flashback Four couldn't stop staring at the figures. Some of them seemed to be crying out in pain.

"Let me show you something else," Miss Z said. She instructed Luke to make a right turn at a street called Vicolo dell'Anfiteatro. One block down were the ruins of a gigantic oval-shaped building.

"It looks like a stadium," David commented.

"It *was* a stadium," Miss Z told him. "This is the

earliest surviving stone amphitheater in the world. It was built in 70 BC. That's a hundred and fifty years before the famous Colosseum in Rome."

"What did they play here?" David asked. "It's not like they had basketball, football, or baseball in those days."

"Their spectator sport was gladiator competitions," Miss Z replied. "Men would face off against each other with weapons. They would fight to the death."

"That is *gross*," Isabel said.

"You're right," Miss Z agreed. "It must have been really gross."

"Hey, which of *you* guys do you think would win a fight to the death?" Julia asked David and Luke.

"Oh, me, definitely," Luke replied right away. "I'm bigger and stronger than David. I would kick his skinny butt nine ways to Sunday."

"I beg to differ," David replied. "It is you, my friend, whose butt would surely be kicked. I am infinitely faster, smoother, and wiser. Like my man Ali, I'd win, you see. I float like a butterfly and sting like a bee."

"The gladiator contests were a *big* deal," Miss Z told the kids. "They were free, and everybody in town would come to see the blood and gore."

"Can we go inside the amphitheater?" asked Isabel.

"I don't think we have time," Miss Z said, looking at her watch. "We need to get back to our meeting spot. We should let Mrs. Vader know. Isabel, will you text her and tell her we're on our way?"

Isabel went to get the TTT out of her backpack, but it wasn't in the pocket where she'd put it.

"Where is it?" asked David, concerned.

"I had it a few minutes ago," Isabel said, quickly opening the other zippered compartments of her backpack.

"That thing cost a fortune," Luke said, looking at Miss Z. "You've got to find it, Isabel. We don't have a lot of time."

"I know! I know!" Isabel said frantically. "I . . . I don't have it anymore. It's gone."

"What do you mean it's gone?" asked Julia. "Check all the pockets."

"I did!" Isabel was on the verge of tears.

"Maybe your backpack was picked!" said Luke, looking around quickly. "We've gotta find the guy who did it."

"He couldn't have gone far," David said.

There were a few dozen tourists in the area. Many of them were holding cell phones, which looked much like the TTT.

"How are we going to know who has it?" asked Isabel.

In Boston, Mrs. Vader's TTT beeped and she looked at the message. . . .

AMERICANS ARE MUTO!

She looked at it twice to make sure she had read it correctly. *Muto* meant "stupid" in Italian. Why would Isabel write a thing like *that*?

IS EVERYTHING ALL RIGHT? Mrs. Vader texted back.

The reply . . .

GEORGE WASHINGTON WAS A LITTLE GIRL.

Mrs. Vader realized immediately that somebody

had pickpocketed Isabel, and the TTT had fallen into the wrong hands. But there was nothing she could do about it.

In Pompeii, the Flashback Four quickly split in two groups, rushing around to peer at the cell phones in the hands of every person in the area. It was a few minutes until David spotted a short teenager with a mohawk haircut holding the TTT, texting and chuckling to himself. David went over and grabbed Luke.

"Over there!" David whispered. "That guy has it!"

The two boys walked purposefully to the teenager with the mohawk, who put his hand behind his back as they approached.

"Excuse me," Luke said politely.

"Buongiorno," the teenager replied.

"I believe you have something that belongs to us," Luke told him.

"No speak English," the guy said.

"Give it back, buddy," David said, holding his hand out.

"I'm not your buddy."

"I thought you didn't speak English," Luke said.

"So I lied," the guy said.

"You *stole* that," accused David, pulling the guy's hand in front of him.

"What is it you Americans say?" the guy said. "Finders keepers, losers weepers?"

"You didn't find it," Luke said, getting closer to the guy's face. "You opened my friend's backpack."

By now, the rest of the group had come over to see what was going on.

"There's no need to fight, boys," Miss Z said as she pulled a twenty-dollar bill out of her purse and held it out to the Italian guy. "Will this be sufficient to make you give that back?"

The guy looked at the bill and then at Miss Z. Twenty US dollars could buy a lot. But he could tell these American tourists wanted the strange cell phone pretty badly. He made the instant calculation in his head that the thing must be worth at least five times what the lady in the wheelchair was offering.

"I'll give it to you for a hundred," he said.

Miss Z started reaching into her purse.

"No way!" Luke said, stopping her.

He got in the guy's face. "You *stole* that. We're not giving you a dime for it."

The Italian teenager stepped back and looked at

Luke from head to toe, sizing him up.

"My friends are on a rugby team," he said. "They will take care of *you*."

"Oh, yeah, I don't see your friends," Luke said, looking around. "Where are they?"

"They will be here very soon," the boy assured him. "Believe me."

"Back off, dude," David told Luke. "Let it go. Miss Z will pay the money."

"Hurry up!" Isabel said, pulling on Luke's elbow. "It's almost one o'clock. If we don't get to the meeting spot soon, we're not going to make it home. That's more important than the TTT."

Luke shook her off. It wasn't the money. It was the principle of the thing. The guy with the mohawk had stolen their TTT. It was in his hand. Luke wasn't going pay a ransom for it.

"Give it back, man," he said, holding his hand out. "*Now*. You don't need it."

"Americans," the guy said dismissively, and then he spit on the ground to emphasize the point.

"How do you know we're Americans?" David asked. "Maybe we're . . . Canadians."

"You think you own the world," the boy replied.

"That's how I know you are Americans."

"We don't own the world," Luke informed the guy. "But we do own *that* thing you're holding. It belongs to us."

"Are you accusing me of stealing?" the guy asked.

"Yes!"

"It's not important, Luke," Miss Z told him. "I can make a new—"

Before she could finish her sentence, Luke made a quick, hard jab with his right hand to the guy's throat and followed it up with a left to his stomach. The guy gasped and doubled over, flipping the TTT a few feet up in the air. David grabbed it before it could hit the ground.

"Thank you!" Luke said with exaggerated gratitude as the guy gasped for breath on his knees. "Okay, let's go."

"Nice move, dude!" David said as they hurried away, genuinely impressed. "You learn that in karate?"

"Yeah," Luke replied. "It was just a video I saw. The element of surprise. Works every time."

The Flashback Four pushed Miss Z's wheelchair hurriedly back down Via dell'Abbondanza and through the Porta Marina gate, to the spot where they had arrived at Pompeii an hour earlier. It was just before one o'clock.

"Okay, everybody get tight," Miss Z instructed, "like you're posing for a picture."

The group squeezed closer together. In the distance, a church bell rang, announcing the hour.

"Hey, look!" Julia shouted, pointing toward the Porta Marina gate.

Five burly guys in rugby shirts were striding purposely in their direction. The guy with the mohawk was in front of them, talking in Italian.

"Oh, shoot!" Luke said.

The rugby players were about twenty feet away and closing.

"What are we going to do *now*?" asked Isabel, putting her hands over her eyes.

Fortunately, the Flashback Four didn't have to do *anything*. At that moment, in the offices of Pasture Company, Mrs. Vader hit the SEND button on her keyboard. The Board lit up in bands of color. In Pompeii, the Flashback Four started flickering.

"Huh?" one of the rugby players said, stopping short a few feet away.

"So long, suckers!" shouted David.

At that moment, the Flashback Four and Miss Z disappeared from Pompeii and reappeared back in Boston.

TOOLS OF THE TRADE

"AHAHAHAHAHA!"

The Flashback Four were in hysterics as they tumbled onto the carpet, nearly knocking down a floor lamp and falling all over each other.

"Did you see the look on that guy's face?" David said, barely able to control himself. "I wish we took a picture of *him*."

"I didn't see it," Isabel cackled. "I had my eyes closed the whole time!"

"They looked like they were gonna kill us!" said Luke.

Even Miss Z couldn't stop herself from giggling a little.

"I want you kids to know that I do not approve of violence in any form," she said, trying to regain her composure. "But that fellow *did* have it coming."

"What happened?" asked Mrs. Vader. "Did you get in trouble over there?"

"No, no," Miss Z assured her. "Everything went perfectly. We had an absolutely *delightful* time in Pompeii. It was just as I remembered it."

"I'm sorry I lost the TTT for a little while," Isabel said.

"You didn't lose it," Luke told her. "That guy was a criminal."

"Oh, who cares, anyway?" Julia bubbled, not wanting to put a damper on the festive mood. "That was *fun*! I haven't had so much fun since . . . since we were on the *Titanic*."

Luke, David, Julia, and Isabel glanced at one another. Each of them had the same thought. Their quick outing to Pompeii had been a blast all around. They had forgotten what pure exhilaration felt like. They had experienced it in Gettysburg and on the *Titanic*. Now they wanted to feel that feeling again. It was almost like an addiction.

But they would have to convince Miss Z. On their first two missions, the Flashback Four had encountered very dangerous, life-threatening situations. She hadn't forgotten that. Even though their little jaunt to Pompeii had worked out, she was still reluctant to send them on another mission.

Isabel, Julia, and David instinctively turned to Luke to be the group spokesman.

"Okay," he said, pulling a chair over so he would be at the same eye level as Miss Z. "You said Mount Vesuvius erupted at noon, right? And the date was . . ."

"August twenty-fourth, in the year 79," Isabel remembered.

"Right," Luke continued. "You said it took a half an hour before all that ash and rock and stuff started falling on Pompeii. So if you were to zap us over there before noon on that day, and zap us back a few minutes *after* noon, we could be back here in time for lunch. What could go wrong?"

"Famous last words," said Miss Z.

"We'll bring back a photo of Mount Vesuvius erupting, for your museum," Luke promised. "Cross my heart and hope to die."

"You can count on us, Miss Z," added Julia. "We're getting good at this."

"Please?" begged David and Isabel.

The Flashback Four looked at Miss Z with their puppy-dog eyes. She could see the yearning in their faces. She could see how they had bonded together as a team. And she had seen with her own eyes how determined and competent they could be in a pressure situation.

"I really shouldn't be doing this," she finally agreed. "But I'll let you go on one more mission."

"Yes!" the kids shouted, high-fiving and clapping each other on the back.

"We're going back to Pompeii!" Julia whooped and shouted triumphantly.

"But I want you kids to know something," Miss Z said seriously, holding her hand up. "A word of warning. This will *not* be like going to Gettysburg or the *Titanic*. This will be almost *prehistoric*. And it will be a *very* different world from what you just saw in modern day Pompeii. Nobody is going to be selling souvenirs and postcards on the street."

"There won't be any pickpockets either," Julia pointed out.

"Oh, I wouldn't be so sure of that," said Miss Z. "There were plenty of bad people in Pompeii back in the year 79 too, I bet. Maybe *worse* people. As always,

I'll need you to stay together at all times and work as a team."

"We always work as a team," David said. "We're the Flashback Four."

David, Luke, Julia, and Isabel went home with instructions to familiarize themselves with Pompeii and the Roman Empire at the time of the Mount Vesuvius eruption. The better prepared they were, the better they would be at handling any unexpected situations. Two days later they came back to Miss Z's office, armed with information and excited to get started on their next mission.

"Well, what have you kids learned?" Miss Z said, clapping her hands together. "How did you conduct your research?"

"I read a book for adults," Isabel said. "It was called *The Fires of Vesuvius*, by Mary Beard."

"Me too," said David. "I think mine was just called *Pompeii* or something."

"I went online," Julia reported. "There are like a zillion websites all about the Roman Empire."

"Good. How about you, Luke?" asked Miss Z. "What did you do?"

"I watched a movie," Luke replied.

"Oh, which one? I *love* film," said Miss Z. "Was it *The Last Days of Pompeii*? That was marvelous. Alan Hale was in it. Did you know that his son played the Skipper in that silly TV series *Gilligan's Island*?"

"The movie I watched was *Animal House*," said Luke.

"*Animal House*?" said David, puzzled. "I saw that movie when I was little. What does it have to do with Pompeii?"

"Not a whole lot," replied Luke. "But there was one scene where all the frat guys dressed up in togas. Will we get to wear togas?"

"To-ga! To-ga! To-ga!" Luke and David began chanting until Miss Z held up her hand.

For those of you who don't know, a toga is a long, loose piece of clothing that was sort of like a bedsheet wrapped around your body.

"I'm sorry," Miss Z told the boys, bringing their chant to a halt. "Only the noblemen in ancient Rome wore togas."

"Oh man," grumbled David. "Togas are cool."

"So what did everybody else wear?" asked Julia.

"I'm glad you asked," replied Miss Z. "Mrs. Vader, will you please go get the clothes we discussed?"

Mrs. Vader went out in the hall.

"Isn't this exciting?" Julia whispered to Isabel. "We're going to be the most fashionable ladies in all of Pompeii!"

Julia loved fashion. Shopping was her favorite thing to do in the world. Nothing made her happier than trying on new clothes.

Mrs. Vader wheeled in a rack of clothes. They were identical formless, shapeless, full-length cotton frocks. Rags, really. It would be almost like wearing a garbage bag with armholes and a hole for the head cut out of it. And they were all the same color—beige. Some had stains on them.

"Those are for the boys, right?" Julia asked hopefully. "After this, you're going to bring out the ladies' clothes for Isabel and me."

"No, these are the clothes for *all* of you," said Mrs. Vader.

Julia couldn't hide her disappointment.

"They're not very fashionable," she said, feeling the material. David and Luke rolled their eyes.

"It's not about being fashionable," Miss Z said. "This is not about making you look good. It's about blending in with the everyday people of Pompeii. This is what regular people wore. Remember, you're going to the year 79. They didn't have factories or sewing machines back then. They didn't have machines of any sort."

Each of the kids picked an outfit off the rack and went to the little changing rooms adjoining Miss Z's office. A few minutes later, David was the first to emerge.

"I'm looking *good*!" he said, showing off for Miss Z and Mrs. Vader. "Hey, we should walk around Boston like this and blow everyone's mind."

Luke came out next, looking pretty much the same as David.

"Well," he said, "it's better than that sailor suit you made me wear on the *Titanic. That* was humiliating."

Isabel was next to emerge from the changing room. She spun around, struck a pose, and pointed one finger in the air.

"'Friends, Romans, countrymen!'" she bellowed. "'Lend me your ears. I come to bury Caesar, not to praise him!'"

Miss Z and Mrs. Vader clapped. The boys just stared at Isabel blankly.

"That's Shakespeare!" Isabel told them. "It's one of the most famous speeches ever given! Didn't you guys read *Julius Caesar* in fifth grade?"

"Julius *who*?" asked David.

"I had a Caesar *salad* in fifth grade," added Luke.

One-fourth of the Flashback Four had yet to emerge from the changing room.

"Come on out, Julia!" called Miss Z.

"No!" Julia shouted back. "This is horrible. I'm staying in here forever."

"Don't be a baby," Isabel said. "We all look the same."

Finally, Julia came out, hiding her face in her hands.

"You look fine," said Mrs. Vader.

"I look like I'm homeless," Julia complained. "If any of my friends saw me dressed like this, I'd have to change schools."

Miss Z informed the kids that even though they were dressed in rags, the people of the Roman Empire considered keeping their clothes clean to be a high priority. When Pompeii was finally unearthed in the 1800s, a dozen laundries were discovered among the ruins.

At that point, Mrs. Vader brought in a tray with bread, cheese, and pastries for the kids to munch on. Julia asked about what foods they should expect to find in Pompeii, but Miss Z told her it shouldn't be an issue.

"I'm sending you there for just two hours," she said. "You shouldn't need to eat a meal. When you get back, I'll give you lunch and you can tell me all about your adventure."

While the kids snacked, Miss Z opened her desk drawer and one by one took out four pieces of technology they would need to complete their new mission....

1. Camera

For the Gettysburg project, Miss Z had given the Flashback Four a complicated digital SLR camera, which was large and hard to use or conceal. That turned out to be a problem. For the *Titanic* mission, she had given them a smaller, simpler point-and-shoot camera. *This* time, Miss Z pulled out what looked to be a standard cell phone.

"It's basically a phone without the phone," she said as she handed it to Luke. "But it has a built-in zoom lens, so you can get a close-up shot of the mountain as it is erupting."

"Any special instructions?" he asked.

"It's simple," Miss Z explained. "As soon as Mount Vesuvius blows and all that rock comes blasting out, just push this button. Then I'll get you out of there before anything hits the ground."

2. Timer

On the first two missions, the kids had been given a watch so they would know what time they needed to get back to the meeting spot for the return trip. But watches have a tendency to get broken, lost, or wet. This time, Miss Z pulled a small digital timer out of her drawer. It was waterproof, and about the size of a matchbook.

"I'm going to set this for a hundred and twenty minutes," she told the kids. "Two hours. That should give you plenty of time to get the lay of the land in Pompeii and find a good location to take the photo. When the timer clicks down to zero, that's when we're going to bring you back here. Unless, of course, you tell me to do it sooner. Got it?"

"Got it," all four agreed.

She handed the timer to David.

"You'll notice that each of you has a small pocket sewn into your frock to hold these devices," Miss Z told the group. "You can thank Mrs. Vader for her fine needlework."

3. TTT

The TTT was Miss Z's pride and joy. Text Through Time. It enabled the Flashback Four to swap texts with her in Boston while they were in a completely different time period. The first TTT cost millions to develop, and it was destroyed. Its replacement was lost on the *Titanic*. Fortunately, after the first one was made, it was a fairly simple matter to build extra units.

"I want to know where you are and what you are doing at all times," Miss Z instructed as she handed the TTT to Isabel. "Do you understand?"

"Yes."

4. Ear Buddies

Before reaching into the drawer one last time, Miss Z had a question for the Flashback Four.

"Do you kids know what language people spoke in Pompeii during the Roman Empire?"

"Uh, Roman?" replied Luke.

"Roman isn't a language, dope!" David said, slapping his friend on the back of the head.

"They spoke Latin," said Isabel, who remembered reading that in the book about Pompeii.

"That's right," said Miss Z.

"I don't even know if the English language *existed* in the year 79," Isabel added. "How are we going to communicate with people when we get to Pompeii?"

"Good question," Miss Z said as she reached into her drawer once more. She pulled out a long, thin box, the sort of box that would hold a new watch. She had a little gleam in her eye as she opened it. Inside were four tiny, flesh-colored objects that looked sort of like the eraser you see at the end of a pencil.

"This is F-R-E-D," she said as she carefully handed one to each of the kids. "It stands for Fully Recognizable English Decoder."

"What does it do?" Luke asked.

"It's a universal translator," Miss Z explained. "It fits inside your ear canal like an earplug. Vocal sounds come in this side. FRED instantly translates the words and repeats them into your ear in English. And when you speak, it translates your words into that language as they come out of your mouth."

"How does it work?" asked Isabel.

"Nanotechnology," Miss Z explained. "It is the science of working with atoms and molecules to build devices that are extremely small. My tech team has been working on this for many years. It has a tiny battery inside. But there are no moving parts, so it doesn't use much energy. And when you put it in your ear like an earplug, it's virtually invisible. Go ahead, try it out."

Luke, Isabel, David, and Julia each inserted a FRED into one ear.

"Hello," said Julia. "Testing . . . one . . . two . . . three."

"You've got to say something in a *foreign* language," Isabel pointed out.

"Bonjour," David said, and instantly the word *hello* echoed in the ears of the others.

"Wow!" said Luke. "That *is* amazing!"

"It can translate virtually every language that has ever been spoken," said Miss Z. "I'm very proud of it, as you might imagine."

"How much did it cost to make that?" asked Isabel.

"You don't want to know," said Miss Z. "I thought about naming it TT for Tiny Translator, but I thought that was too close to the TTT. Then I thought about naming it LISTEN, for Language Interpretation System Translator & Ear Nano-Robotic. But I decided to go with FRED instead. It's friendlier, don't you think?"

"It's sort of like a translating earbud," said David. "Hey, you should call it Ear Buddy!"

"Ear Buddies!" exclaimed Miss Z. "I *like* that!"

"Okay, is that it?" asked Luke, whose patience for sitting still had just about come to its end. "Can we go to Pompeii now?"

"Everybody should use the bathroom before you leave," said Mrs. Vader.

"You sound like my mother," Julia said.

"I don't have to go to the bathroom," said Luke.

"Try to go anyway," instructed Miss Z. "They're not going to have regular toilets—or toilet paper—when you get to Pompeii. Do you want to know what they used during the Roman Empire instead?"

"Uh . . . I'm not sure I want to know," said Isabel.

"A sponge mounted on a stick," Miss Z said. That was followed by a chorus of gagging noises from the Flashback Four. "They would dip it into a bucket of salt water or vinegar water—"

"Okay, okay! TMI!" shouted the kids as they rushed to the bathroom.

When they got back, Luke, Isabel, David, and Julia took their places in front of the Board. It was 10:15 a.m. Mrs. Vader took David's timer and set it for 120 minutes—two hours.

"Exactly two hours from now, at 12:15, I need you four to be outside the Porta Marino gate at Pompeii," Miss Z instructed the team. "Do you remember where it is? That's the same spot where we landed the first time."

"We'll be there," Luke said. "We promise."

Mrs. Vader woke up the computer and turned on the Board to warm it up.

"One last thing," Miss Z told the group. "I know you kids. You like to fix things. You may very well feel a desire to right a wrong, to prevent a death, or change history in some way. When we see a stranger about to walk into the path of a moving car, we reach out and pull them back. It's human nature. That's the way our brains are wired. And it's a good thing. That's probably why our civilization has survived. But your job here is *not* to do good deeds. Your job is to take a photograph. You are photojournalists. Do you understand?"

"We understand."

"Any people you interact with in Pompeii are almost certainly going to die. Do *not* become friends with them. Do *not* become emotionally attached to them. And by all means, do *not* try to rescue them. Got it?"

"Got it," said David. "We promise to be totally cold and heartless."

"Okay, let's get this show on the road," Luke said.

By this time, the Flashback Four had become accustomed to the way the Board worked. They no longer needed to be told to brace themselves, or to close their eyes. They knew the routine.

So do you.

Miss Z cranked up the Board. It did its thing.

In seconds, the kids were gone.

A NEW OLD CITY

THE FLASHBACK FOUR TUMBLED TO THE GROUND ten feet outside the Porta Marina gate, frightening a couple of goats that had been lolling around in the dirt. Luckily, there were no human beings standing nearby to ask the kids who they were and how they got there.

"Is everybody in one piece?" Luke asked as he stood up and dusted himself off. "Looks like we made it safe and sound."

"Okay, this is the meeting spot," Isabel reminded the others. "If we get separated for any reason, we'll meet up again right here to get back home."

David took out the timer. The screen read 119 minutes, and it was counting down by seconds.

"We've got two hours," he told the others. "Plenty of time to scope out the town and find the perfect location to take the picture. Let's go."

"First I should let Miss Z know we arrived safely," Isabel said, pulling the TTT out of her pocket. She typed into the device. . . .

WE R HERE

Soon, a reply came back. . . .

FANTASTIC! KEEP ME POSTED.

It was hot out, close to ninety-five degrees. Luke was already sweating. He wiped his forehead with his sleeve and checked the camera. Everything seemed to be in working order.

The Flashback Four were ready to get to work.

Before walking through the entrance to the city, the kids turned around to get a good look at the main attraction—Mount Vesuvius. It looked very different than it had the first time they visited. It was much higher now. The top of the mountain hadn't blown off yet.

"In two hours, it's going to erupt, and all that rock is going to go flying," David said. "Less than twenty-four hours from now, the people who are still inside these walls are going to be dead."

It was a sobering thought. Those plaster casts they had seen on the first trip were the same people who were walking around Pompeii right now.

"Don't even *think* about it, dude," Luke told David. "It's out of our hands. We can't save them."

"This time, I'm just worried about saving *myself*," said Julia.

GOING THROUGH PORTA MARINA GATE, Isabel typed into the TTT.

There were no iron gates, pizza parlors, or souvenir sellers this time. Instead, there was one burly guard wearing a helmet and armor and holding a sword. He looked the kids over as they passed by, but didn't stop them or say anything. People seemed to be allowed to move freely in and out of the city. Or maybe the guards just didn't hassle kids.

As they walked through the gate, the Flashback Four stopped in their tracks. Pompeii looked familiar, but very different. The ruins weren't . . . ruined. The buildings were taller, newer, more colorful, and they had *roofs* on them. This time, everything was *alive*.

Pompeii was a bustling port city, buzzing with

activity. The harbor was just a quarter of a mile away. The kids instantly recognized the main road they had walked down previously, Via dell'Abbondanza, even though there were no street signs. But this time it wasn't filled with blue-jeaned, baseball-capped, picture-snapping tourists who would be going back to their air-conditioned hotel rooms that night. The people on the street actually lived and worked in Pompeii.

There were shoemakers, bakers, greengrocers, weavers, gem cutters, and barbers. There were mat makers, ointment sellers, and chicken keepers. All over the street, people were hawking stuff from stores and makeshift stalls. Many were selling and buying *garum*, a fish sauce that was considered a specialty of Pompeii. Merchants rushed around carrying their wares in baskets, carts, and jugs. Many had the help of donkeys, mules, and horses. You could buy just about anything here, from Far East spices to an African monkey.

There were lots of nice smells in the air—bread, olive oil, grapes, and roses from perfume makers. Fish frying. Oh, and a whiff of urine.

It was great people-watching. A group of men were kneeling down, playing a dice game. Street mimes acted out stories, trying to attract an audience that might throw them a coin or two. A musician played a lyre—a small harp that looks like a little guitar. Beggars asked for handouts. Some kids were playing a game that looked like handball. Most of the people on the street were men. Women were not allowed to vote or hold power in ancient Rome. A few older women fanned themselves to keep cool as they gossiped on a corner.

"Man, these guys are *short*," David said, and it was true. The average male during the Roman Empire stood about five feet tall. The Flashback Four towered over most of the people on the street.

The timer counted down: 116 minutes.

The kids stood and watched the action swirl around them for a few minutes. Everything seemed so much more colorful than it had been the first time they were there—bright whites, deep reds, vivid yellows. The mosaics and paintings on the walls of buildings looked fresh and new. At the intersection, street fountains bubbled with water.

"*E pluribus unum,*" Isabel said to a smiling old man pushing a cart.

"*E pluribus unum,*" the man replied.

"*E pluribus unum,*" she said to a lady carrying a large jug on her head.

"E pluribus unum," the lady replied.

"Why are you saying that to everybody?" asked Julia.

"It's the only Latin I know," Isabel replied. "It means 'Out of many, one.'"

"Where did you learn Latin?" asked Luke.

"I didn't. It says *'e pluribus unum'* on the back of every quarter."

"Who reads the writing on quarters?" asked David.

"Me," Isabel replied.

"You don't need to do that, you know," Julia told her. "We have the Ear Buddy, remember?"

"Oh, yeah!"

The Ear Buddy that was in each of their ears took a little getting used to. The Flashback Four sidled over near two men standing on the corner in order to eavesdrop on the conversation.

"I fear the heat may ruin this year's harvest," one of the men said to his friend, in Latin.

A millisecond after he said that, the kids heard those words in their ears—in English.

"Be hopeful, citizen," said the other man. "I feel the cool winds will arrive this evening."

"It works!" Isabel whispered to the others. "Did you hear that? They're talking about how hot it is today."

"I can't believe grown-ups made small talk about the weather back in the year 79," said Julia.

"Some things never change," David remarked.

Emboldened, Julia skipped off down the street, making meaningless chitchat in Latin with every passerby she encountered.

"Nice day we're having," she said to a bearded man with a cane.

"Lovely," he replied.

"They say it may rain on Friday," she said to another man.

"That would be good for the crops," he replied.

Luke, David, and Isabel rushed to catch up with her. They weren't about to let Julia get too far ahead. She had a history of running off to go on little adventures of her own.

"Latin is *fun*!" she told them.

"Hey, check this out," Luke said. He walked over to a bald man carrying a dog and asked him, "What do you think of the Red Sox?"

The bald man looked at his feet, and then back at Luke.

"The color of my socks does not much matter to me," he replied.

The Flashback Four cracked up.

"Whew, you should have smelled the breath on that guy," Luke told the others. "These Romans need to invent toothpaste, fast."

LUKE JUST ASKED A GUY IF HE LIKED THE RED SOX! Isabel typed on the TTT.

Miss Z replied a few seconds later with a smiley-face emoji.

"Y'know, we should make sure we got here on the right day," David told the group. "Remember what happened in Gettysburg."

Ah yes, Gettysburg. Due to a typo by Miss Z, the Flashback Four arrived in Gettysburg one day early, the day *before* Abraham Lincoln's famous speech. That caused all kinds of problems.

"We need to find a newspaper," Julia said, looking around for a garbage can. "You can always find one in the garbage."

"They don't have newspapers in the year 79!" Luke told her, rolling his eyes. "I don't even know if they have garbage cans."

David took matters into his own hands, walking up to a man with a dog on a leash.

"Excuse me, sir," he said politely, "is today Tuesday, August twenty-fourth, in the year 79?"

The man looked at David blankly for a moment.

Miss Z had told the kids that ancient Romans used a calendar similar to ours. Saturday was named for the planet Saturn. Sunday was named for the sun, and Monday for the moon.

"It is certainly the twenty-fourth day of the month August," the man replied. "But what do you mean by the year 79? This is the first year of the reign of Emperor Titus Vespasianus Augustus! Hail Emperor Titus!"

"Hail Titus!" chanted a few passersby.

"Okay, okay, chill," said David.

AUGUST 24 CONFIRMED, Isabel typed into the TTT.

The timer counted down: 113 minutes.

The first time they were in Pompeii, the streets were just about bare. Museums had snatched up most of the statues and artifacts that were found when the city was dug up. But this time, statues were all over the place. Every few yards was another large marble representation of a Roman god, emperor, or hero— Jupiter, king of the gods and guardian of the state. Venus, the goddess of love. Mars, the god of war. And of course, the emperor Titus.

As the Flashback Four meandered down Via dell'Abbondanza, they could see there were cracks in the walls of many of the stores and houses. Seventeen years earlier, in the year 62, a violent earthquake had swept through the region and reduced much of Pompeii to rubble. The town was still getting back on its feet.

Also on the walls were lots of advertisements, political campaign posters, and graffiti. The kids couldn't read the Latin words, but they stopped to examine them anyway. . . .

A copper pot went missing from my shop. Anyone who returns it to me will be given sixty-five bronze coins.

Health to you, Victoria, and wherever you are may you sneeze sweetly.

Cruel Lalagus, why do you not love me?

Let him perish who knows not love. Let him perish twice over whoever forbids love.

"I wonder what they say," David said.

"They look sort of like ancient texts or tweets," said Julia. That reminded Isabel to keep Miss Z informed of their whereabouts every step of the way.

HAVING A GREAT TIME, Isabel typed on the TTT. WISH YOU WERE HERE.

On the wall of one building was a poster with a picture of two men fighting. Even though the Flashback Four couldn't make out the words, it looked like an advertisement for an upcoming gladiator competition.

Below the poster, somebody had scribbled, in Latin: *Celadus, glory of the girls, heartthrob of the girls!*

"I can't believe that people actually wasted time watching men intentionally hurt each other," Isabel said. "That's so barbaric."

"Ever hear of professional boxing?" Luke asked her. "Or wrestling? Or mixed martial arts? We still have the same stuff."

"Those things are barbaric too," Isabel replied.

The timer counted down: 111 minutes.

One thing that surprised the kids was the number of restaurants in Pompeii. (Over a hundred fifty, according to historians.) Just about every other storefront was selling food. It was late morning, so some people were eating an early lunch—fish, cold meat, carrots, cucumbers, or other veggies. Others were just finishing up breakfast—bread or a wheat pancake with dates and honey. The poor ate simply, while rich people chowed down on luxuries we would consider exotic: boar, wild goat, ostriches, cranes, doves, roasted peacock, and stork tongue. And wine, of course. Lots of wine.

"Eat, drink, and be merry," hollered a baker in front of his little shop, "for tomorrow you may die."

"He doesn't know how right he is," David said.

"Nobody is selling pizza," Luke noticed. "How could they not have pizza here?"

"I don't think pizza has been invented yet," guessed Isabel.

In fact, it would be more than nine hundred years before anything called "pizza" would be eaten *anywhere* in the world.

"This stuff looks good," Luke said, pointing to some meat on a stick. "I'm getting hungry."

"You're *always* hungry," noted Julia.

"Maybe we should ask them for some food," suggested Isabel.

"Nah, let 'em enjoy it," David told her. "This will be their last meal."

The timer counted down: 109 minutes.

EVERYTHING GOING SMOOTHLY, Isabel typed on the TTT.

LOOKING FOR PERFECT PHOTO LOCATION.

They turned a corner onto a little side street, only to be surprised by a disturbing sight. A man was whipping another man with a long stick. The guy getting whipped already had some dark lines on his back.

"Forty-five! Forty-six! Forty-seven!" shouted the man who was doing the whipping. "How many lashes will teach you to behave, slave?"

Slave?

When we think of slavery, we usually think of what happened in our own country before the Civil War. But slavery was an accepted part of life during the Roman Empire. More than a third of the people in Pompeii were slaves.

It was hard for the kids to watch a man getting beaten. Nobody was coming over to stop it. People on the street just walked by without seeming to notice anything unusual going on.

"Maybe we should help that guy," Isabel said.

"No!" Luke told her. "That's not what we're here for, remember?"

The timer counted down: 107 minutes.

The kids continued wandering the streets, looking for the right spot to take their photo of Mount Vesuvius. There were a lot of dogs roaming around too, some with their owners and some without. There were no pooper scooper laws, obviously.

"Watch where you step," Julia instructed the others. "Remember Gettysburg."

Oh, yes. In Gettysburg the streets were filled with horses, which meant the streets were filled with horse manure. Julia had found this out the hard way.

Just to be on the safe side, she was staring down at the street in front of her, being careful to avoid stepping into anything unpleasant. That's when a woman shouted from her second-story balcony above.

"Watch out below!"

David looked up quickly and saw that the woman overhead had tipped a bucket and was pouring something out onto the street. He gave Julia a hard shove to push her out of the way just before she would have been drenched with raw sewage.

"What the—did she just—?" Julia sputtered. "I can't believe she—That is so gross and disgusting! Why would a human being *do* that?"

Isabel was grossed out too, but the boys—being boys—found it hysterical, especially when Julia almost stepped in dog poop right after avoiding the flying pee.

"I thought the Romans were famous for their

indoor plumbing," Isabel said.

"I guess everybody didn't have indoor plumbing," David told her.

"I don't care that they don't have it!" Julia exclaimed, unable to calm down. "You don't throw the contents of your toilet out the window! It's just not done!"

"Calm down," Luke told her. "You didn't get a drop on you. Look, we'll be out of here in less than two hours. Then we can go home to our indoor plumbing while all these people will have to deal with a lot worse than flying pee."

David checked the timer. 104 minutes.

Any concerns about flying pee or stepping in poop vanished when there was a sudden odd rumbling sound in the air. The street vibrated for a few seconds. The Flashback Four stopped.

"Is that *it*?" asked David nervously. "Is the volcano about to erupt?"

"What if Miss Z got the timing wrong?" Julia said, a frightened look on her face. "Maybe Vesuvius is going to blow early!"

"I don't think so," Isabel said. "In the days leading up to the eruption, there was a series of tremors and small earthquakes in Pompeii."

"How do you know that?" Luke asked.

"I read it in a book," Isabel told him. "You might want to get one sometime. You know, they're these things with lots of pages and writing on them."

"I'm still nervous," David said. "We'd better find a good spot to take the photo. Then, as soon as the volcano erupts, we'll get our shot and be ready to get out of here."

"Good thinking," Luke agreed.

Those words were barely out of Luke's mouth when a voice from behind shouted, "Seize them!"

That's when four thick, hairy arms reached around and grabbed the Flashback Four by the necks.

SHUT YOUR MOUTH!

THE ELEMENT OF SURPRISE. IT HAD WORKED PER-fectly for the Flashback Four when they needed to get the TTT back from that obnoxious pickpocket on their first visit to Pompeii. And it worked perfectly *against* them now. As a weapon, just about nothing is as effective as the element of surprise.

"What the—"

Four big guys had jumped Luke, David, Isabel, and Julia before they had the chance to react, over-powering the kids. With a muscular arm wrapped around each of their throats, the kids were helpless. It wouldn't take much for any of these guys to give one good yank and snap a neck.

"Owww!"

"Get your filthy hands off me!"

"That hurts!"

"What's going on?"

Their attackers didn't say a word. The Flashback Four struggled to bite and kick, but it didn't take long to realize it was useless to fight back. Before they knew what was happening, the kids were being dragged down the street and around the corner.

"What did we do?" David asked. "We didn't hurt anybody!"

"Where are you taking us?" said Luke. "What are you doing?"

"We don't have any money!" Isabel shouted. "We don't have anything at all."

"Shut your mouth, slave!" Isabel's attacker yelled at her.

"Slave?" said Isabel. "We're not slaves!"

"This is a big mistake!" Julia shouted. "My father works for Verizon!"

"Shut up!" one of the thugs shouted.

Julia managed to get one arm free. Her attacker grabbed her roughly and slapped her.

"How *dare* you!" she screamed.

The Flashback Four were dragged across a bumpy stone street, trying to keep their wits about them. Luke tried to memorize the street they had turned on, so he would be able to retrace his steps when—and if—they were able to get free. His attacker smelled bad. He was overpowering in more ways than one.

Luke, David, and Isabel stopped protesting, but Julia was indignant.

"I have my rights!" she shouted. "You're going to be in serious trouble, mister! This is a free country!"

It actually *wasn't* truly a free country. It was a republic, and Emperor Titus had the final say. But let's not get bogged down with *that* stuff. The Flashback Four are getting kidnapped!

There were other people out and about, but nobody seemed to pay any attention to the fact that four kids were being dragged through the street in broad daylight. It was nothing unusual. Slaves received this kind of treatment all the time.

"Call 911!" Julia shouted out to anyone who might be listening. "Hey, aren't we allowed one phone call?"

"There are no phones here, you dope!" Luke muttered to her. "They won't have phones for centuries!"

"Not even landlines?" Julia asked.

Isabel had begun to cry. Of the four kids, she was

the one who was the least prepared to handle stress-ful situations like this. Her parents had raised her very carefully, protecting her from the dangers of the outside world. So when she did encounter a problem or crisis, she was the most likely to freak out or shut down completely.

"They're going to whip us," Isabel sobbed, "just like they whipped that slave on the street!"

"You will not be whipped if you do as we say," the guy with his arm around her neck told her.

"Where are you taking us?" David demanded of his attacker. "We haven't done anything wrong, and we aren't slaves."

"Didn't you hear me the first time, slave?" the thug replied, slapping David in the face. "I said shut up!"

It was a hopeless situation. Luke knew it would be up to him to get them out of it. He leaned over and tried to whisper to Isabel.

"If you can get a hand free," he whispered, "try to send a text."

Of course! If they could let Miss Z know the situation they were in, she could zap them back to Boston. They wouldn't get the photo of Mount Vesuvius, of course, but at least they would be able to get away from these thugs. Isabel struggled to get an arm free to pull the TTT out of her pocket.

"I can't reach it!" she groaned.

David saw what was going on. He figured a diversionary tactic might give Isabel the chance to get out the TTT.

"So," he said to the thugs, "could you guys use some money? I have a hundred gold coins that are yours if you let us go."

Luke shot David a look. He knew that David didn't have any coins.

The thugs stopped.

"Where are these coins of which you speak?" one of them said.

"I'll bring you to them," David said. "Just take your arm off my neck."

The four thugs shot each other glances, and one by one loosened their grip on the Flashback Four.

"That's better," David said, rubbing his neck.

"Now take us to the coins," one thug demanded.

"Yeah, uh, sure . . ." David looked around. "Now let me see. I think I left them around the corner over there. . . ."

While David was trying to distract the thugs, Isabel hurriedly reached into her pocket for the TTT. She got it out, but in her haste to send a message, she lost her grip and it fell, clattering to the stone street below.

"What's this?" one of the thugs asked, snatching the TTT up off the ground before Isabel could grab it.

"Nothing," Isabel told him. "Please can I have it back?"

"Sure," the thug said, putting the TTT on the ground again. Then he stomped on it heavily with his boot heel, crushing it.

"No!" shouted the Flashback Four in horror.

"You broke it!" Isabel shouted. "I can't believe you did that!"

The thugs laughed. One of them picked the TTT up off the ground and handed the pieces to Isabel as if he was giving her a gift.

The TTT was destroyed. Once again, the Flashback Four had managed to lose their link to contact Miss Z in Boston. Isabel started bawling, and who could blame her?

"Where are the gold coins?" one of the thugs demanded.

"I . . . uh . . . give me a minute to think . . . maybe . . . ," David stammered.

"These slaves have no coins," shouted one of the

thugs. "We are not fools!"

Now angrier than ever, they grabbed the kids, even more roughly this time, and dragged them down the street.

"What are we going to do *now*?" whispered Julia.

"I'll think of something," Luke assured her.

"Think fast," said David.

They came to an open doorway. The four thugs pushed the kids through it and down a staircase into a basement area. The walls were made of rough stone. There was nothing in the room except for two pairs of chains attached to each of the four walls. It looked like a dungeon.

No, strike that. It didn't look like a dungeon. It *was* a dungeon.

The thugs took Luke, who they correctly perceived to be their biggest threat, and pushed him against the wall. While one thug forced his arms up in the air, two of the other thugs wrapped iron chains around his wrists and snapped them in place with two locks. After Luke's arms had been secured, the same was done with his legs, pushed wide apart. He was spread-eagle with his back against the wall, unable to move more than an inch or two in any direction.

"Is this really necessary?" Luke complained as

the thugs pushed David against the opposite wall and did the same thing to him. Then they turned to Isabel and Julia, chaining them to the other two walls of the room. So each of the walls had a member of the Flashback Four chained to it.

"That should hold 'em," one of the thugs said as the last chain was clicked into place on Julia's ankle. With that, the thugs began to file out of the dungeon.

"Really? You're leaving now?" Julia asked. "*This* is how you treat innocent people in the Roman Empire? Didn't you people invent democracy?"

"I think that was the Greeks," Isabel muttered.

"History is *not* going to judge you people kindly," Julia shouted after the thugs. "Your empire is going to collapse, mark my words."

"Yeah," David added. "I take back all those nice things I said about the Romans in that social studies report I wrote in third grade."

"Stop talking, slaves!" hollered the last thug to leave the dungeon. Then he slammed the heavy door behind him. The lock clicked shut from the other side.

Quiet is a strange sound. We hear it so rarely. After the thugs left, the only noise that could be heard in the dungeon was the sound of heavy breathing from Luke,

Isabel, Julia, and David. No words were spoken. Their chains rattled whenever they moved.

It took a few minutes for their eyes to adjust to the dark. On the walls of the dungeon were a couple of bronze oil lamps, but they weren't lit. The only illumination was a small patch of daylight that came through an iron grate in the ceiling. There were no electric lights in the year 79, of course.

"My heart is pounding," David said, finally breaking the silence.

"I can't believe this is happening," said Isabel. "I feel like I must be in the middle of a bad dream, and I'm going to wake up any minute in my bed at home."

She was on the verge of losing it. Luke pushed against the chains that were wrapped around his wrists. There was no give.

"I didn't know they had the technology to make iron in the year 79," he said, grunting from the effort. "I figured people sort of lived like cavemen in these times."

The dungeon was damp and musty. Scary-looking insects crawled around on the dirt floor. In the distance, the sound of people being whipped and tortured could be heard.

"That's what they're going to do to *us* soon," Isabel said, breaking down in tears. It wasn't long until the other three were in various stages of crying, sobbing, and holding it in.

"Any bright ideas?" David asked Luke.

"Yeah," Luke replied. Then he started shouting, "Help! Let us out! Can anybody hear me?"

"Shut up!" a distant voice hollered back. It was unclear whether it was the voice of a guard or somebody who was being guarded.

"I'm sorry, you guys," Isabel said, pulling herself together. "I shouldn't have been holding the TTT. I should have given it to one of you."

"It could have happened to anybody," David told her. "You had to try. That counts for something."

Luke continued to look for an escape route, even though there was clearly no way out. It was his nature—find a problem, fix the problem.

"I *knew* this trip was a dumb idea," Julia said. "What were we thinking? We should have quit while we were ahead, after we survived the *Titanic*."

"If I recall, you were complaining that your life back home was boring after we got back from the *Titanic*. Remember?" David told her. "Well, are you bored *now*?"

When something goes wrong in a group, there's a natural tendency to blame somebody.

"Whose idea was this, anyway?" Luke asked.

"Not me," Isabel replied. "I didn't want to do this."

"I said we should go back to 1776 and take a picture of the Founding Fathers signing the Declaration of Independence," David said. "If we had done that, we wouldn't be in this mess."

"I didn't want to do this," Isabel said. "That's what I get for giving in to peer pressure."

"*You're* the big leader," Julia said to Luke. "So maybe you should take the blame."

"Hey, if it weren't for Luke, you'd still be in the Atlantic Ocean right now!" David barked at her.

"Look, stop it, you guys!" Luke told the group. "This is ridiculous! We were all in agreement that we wanted to do this. So it's nobody's fault. Let's stop playing the blame game and think of a way out of here."

"Way out of here?" Julia said with a laugh. "Are you kidding? We're chained to the *wall* in a locked dungeon. The volcano is going to blow in less than two hours, and we're going to die in here. Can you come up with a solution to *that*?"

"What do you think they're going to do with us?" Isabel asked.

"Nothing," David replied. "They'll just leave us here. Nobody will find us for a couple of thousand years. Then they'll pour liquid plaster into the empty cavities where our dead bodies used to be."

David started thinking about his dogs back home. He had three beagles—Moe, Larry, and Curly—and they were the love of his life. David had always been an animal lover, and the thought of never seeing his dogs again pushed him over the edge. He started crying, and couldn't wipe the tears away.

"Will you *stop* it?" Luke scolded him. "We're not going to be dead bodies. We'll find a way out of this. We always do. Remember Gettysburg? Remember *Titanic*? We thought we were in trouble. We thought it was all over. But we found a way out. You've got to think positively."

"I'm thinking that we're positively going to die," David sobbed.

A few minutes passed while everybody tried to cool off.

"How much time do we have left?" Isabel asked.

"I don't know," David replied. "I can't reach the timer."

In his pocket, the timer counted down: 99 minutes.

"I'm hungry," Julia said.

"How can you think about food?" Isabel asked. "We're going to die here!"

"My stomach is growling," Julia claimed. Then she shouted, "Guard! Guard!"

There were some footsteps outside the door, and then it opened. One of those thugs appeared.

"What do you want?" he asked gruffly.

"We're hungry," Julia replied. "Can we have something to eat, please?"

The thug looked at the four of them and left the room without closing the door. A minute later he came back, holding a plate with some kind of meat on it. He went over to Luke first.

"You need to keep up your strength," the thug told him.

"Do you have a fork?" Luke asked.

"A *what*?"

Luke had no idea that he would have to wait several centuries for the fork to be invented. The Romans ate mainly with their fingers.

Even if they *had* forks, there was no way the guard was going to give Luke one. A fork could be used as a weapon.

The thug put a piece of meat into Luke's mouth. He accepted it gratefully.

"Hey, *I'm* the one who asked for food," Julia complained. "Why are you giving it to him?"

"Quiet over there!" the thug replied. He went over to David with the plate.

"No thank you," David said. "That stuff looks gross."

"You need to keep up your strength," the thug told him.

"How come *they* need to keep up their strength but *we* don't?" complained Isabel. "It's not fair. What, are women second-class citizens around here?"

In fact, women *were* second-class citizens around there.

"Shut your mouth, wench!" the thug barked at her.

Meanwhile, he gave Luke a second piece of meat, which he chewed vigorously.

"Mmm, not bad," Luke said. "What is this, chicken?"

"No, it is dormice," said the thug, "sweetened with honey and sprinkled with poppy seeds."

"It's good," Luke said. "Crunchy. I kind of like this dormice stuff."

"It's a *mouse*, you dope!" Julia said from across the room. "You're eating a *mouse*."

Luke stopped chewing for a moment. Then he started in chewing again.

"That's good mouse," he said.

"Oh, gross!" Isabel exclaimed. "I think I'm going to throw up."

"Guard, is dormice really mouse?" asked Luke.

"Yes. Dormice is mouse. It is stuffed."

"Stuffed with what?" asked Luke.

"Another dormouse, of course."

"No wonder it's so crunchy," Luke said. "You really need to try this, David."

"I don't think so," his friend replied. "I'm on a strict no-mouse diet."

"Stupid slave," said the thug as he left the room and locked the door behind him. "A smart slave would give *anything* for a dormouse."

A few minutes passed. It didn't look like the guard would be coming back any time soon. Time was running out. Even Luke was losing confidence.

"I think this might be the end of the line, you guys," he said solemnly. "In an hour or so, Mount Vesuvius is going to blow its top. Miss Z will try to bring us back home, but we won't be at the meeting spot. If those goats are still there, she'll be in for a surprise. And when that happens, I guess, we're cooked. In more ways than one."

"I never thought it would end this way," Isabel said softly.

"We've been through a lot together," Luke said. "I just want to say I love you guys."

"I love you too, man," David replied. "I thought you were kind of a jerk when we first met, but everything is different now."

"Will you two knock it off?" Julia shouted. "I liked it better when boys didn't have feelings."

This discussion came to an abrupt end when the door suddenly swung open with a loud squeak that startled the Flashback Four. Two of the thugs had come back.

"Slaves!" the taller one shouted. "Come with us!"

"Well, it's about time," Julia said grumpily. "What's the name of your supervisor? I'm going to write a strongly worded letter of complaint—"

"Not *you*," the thug told her. "Just the males. Come with us."

"What?!" both girls exclaimed.

The thugs unchained the boys and grabbed them by the elbows.

"Where are you taking us *now*?" David asked.

"You will see," one of the thugs grunted.

"Hey, what about *us*?" Julia shouted after them. "We don't want to stay here all by ourselves!"

The thugs weren't listening. They dragged Luke

and David out of the dungeon.

As they were escorted away, Luke shouted back at the girls, "If you're able to get free, head for the meeting spot."

LET'S PUT ON A SHOW

THE THUGS PULLED LUKE AND DAVID UP THE steps and out onto the street. Both boys shielded their eyes. It was almost eleven o'clock in the morning now, and the sun was high in the sky. If they hadn't been blinded, it would have been tempting to make a break for it.

Right outside was a wooden vehicle, with a horse tethered to it. It was almost the size of a bus, like a giant cage on wheels. Through the bars the boys saw a group of men, sitting sullenly and not speaking. They looked tired, disheveled, and beaten down.

A red-haired man hopped off the horse that was

pulling the wagon. He had a whip in his hand, which he used to control the horse as well as the men in the cage. He opened a door on the side.

"Climb in, slaves!"

"Look, buddy, we're not slaves," Luke said, speaking quickly before he could be slapped or beaten. "You've got to listen to me. Mount Vesuvius is going to erupt in a little more than an hour. I know. Don't ask me how. I just know. Instead of hassling us, you should be evacuating the whole town. It's going to be buried under twenty feet of ash. Everybody's going to die."

The red-haired man let out a laugh.

"You would make a good storyteller, slave!" he said. "What is your name?"

"Luke."

"I mean, what do they call you?"

"They call me Luke. That's my name."

"That is no kind of name," said the red-haired man. "From now on, your name is Oceanus. I have named you in honor of the god of the waters."

Next he turned to David.

"And what is the name they call you, slave?" he asked.

"My name is David."

"From now on, your name is Hilarius."

"What!" David exclaimed. "Hilarius?"

"That is what I said. You are Hilarius."

"That's a great name, dude," said Luke. "I always thought you were Hilarius."

"Why can't you just call us by our regular names?" asked David.

"Do not question me, slave!" shouted the red-haired man. "Do you want fifty lashes?"

"Eyelashes?" asked David.

"No, idiot! A flogging!"

He took his whip and held it menacingly in front of David. Luke climbed into the wagon, with David right behind him.

"The top of the mountain is going to explode!" Luke shouted. "You've got to believe me!"

"Enough wild talk," the red-haired man said as he calmly closed and locked the door. Then he climbed up on the horse and used his whip to urge it forward.

It was a bumpy, uncomfortable ride through the streets. There were no seats in the wagon, and no padding. The red-haired man, who the boys quickly nicknamed "Fred the Red," guided it through an alley-way called Via di Nocera.

Out on the street, people were pointing and laughing at the wagon, as if they were watching animals in a zoo. A few spit at them.

"Where are you taking us?" David shouted at Fred the Red.

"You will find out in good time, Hilarius."

"My name is *David*!"

Luke turned to look at the ragged man sitting next to him. His hair was messed up, and when he smiled it was obvious that most of his teeth were missing. He smelled bad.

"My name is Crustus," the toothless man said, shaking hands with both of the boys. "I heard what you said about Vesuvius, and I believe you. Giants roam the land near the mountain. They make the ground move, and the giants are angry."

"That guy is crazy," David whispered in Luke's ear.

"I'm not sure about that," Luke whispered back. "Maybe *everybody* here thinks that way. They don't have science. All they have is superstition."

David leaned over toward Crustus.

"Are you a slave?" he asked.

"No. I am a criminal," Crustus replied.

"What did you do?"

"I stole a man's pig."

"Why did you do that?" Luke asked.

"I was hungry."

"What about you guys?" David said to the other prisoners. "Are you criminals too?" They nodded their heads.

"Arson," one of them said.

"Banditry," said another.

"Treason."

"Refusal to pledge loyalty to the emperor."

"Prisoner of war."

Luke and David looked at each other, more confused than ever. Why had they been separated from the girls and thrown in with these guys? Maybe they were being taken to a dungeon just for men. Or maybe they were being taken to be executed.

"Are they going to kill us?" Luke asked Crustus.

"You could say that," Crustus replied.

David sank back in his gloom, putting his hands over his eyes.

"Look on the bright side," Luke told him. "We got out of that dungeon. Now we'll have a chance to escape and save the girls."

The wagon made its way toward the southeast edge of the town. David checked the timer. There were 85 minutes left. Still plenty of time to escape and get back to the meeting spot. The wagon turned a corner and the Pompeii amphitheater came into view.

It was by far the largest structure in town. The boys recognized it from their previous trip. It looked pretty much the same, except that above the top row flags were flying.

"Wow," David marveled, looking up at the big building. "How do you think they built this place without machines and cranes and stuff?"

"Probably with slaves and condemned prisoners," Luke replied. "Maybe that's why we're here. Maybe they're going to make us work here."

Outside the amphitheater, the wagon passed a line of statues of Roman gods and emperors on pedestals. It stopped there. People were waiting in a long line that snaked back and forth leading up to the entrance. The men, women, and children waiting in line looked excited to be there.

"Hey, maybe they're taking us to see one of those gladiator shows," David guessed.

"Oh, you'll get to see a gladiator show all right," Crustus told them. "You'll have the best seat in the house."

"Do you mean . . ."

It took a few moments, but finally the boys realized what was going on. They weren't being taken on some field trip to be entertained at a gladiator show. They were going to *be* the gladiator show!

"Oh, shoot," cursed Luke.

The wagon was wheeled around to the side of the amphitheater, where there was a large courtyard called the Palestra Grande. It was sort of like an open-air dressing room where the gladiators could train and practice while they were waiting for their battle to begin. Brick walls surrounded the area to prevent escape. Several grumpy guards stood in front of the gates with big swords and angry looks on their faces.

"We gotta get out of here, man," Luke whispered to David. "These people are *crazy*. They're gonna make us battle to the *death*. That's what they did in the old days. I saw it in a movie."

It was basically true. While *all* gladiators didn't die fighting, a good many of them did.

"I have an idea," David whispered to Luke. "They gotta give us swords or something to fight with, right? As soon as they hand us our weapons, let's make a run for the gate. If anybody tries to stop us, we use the weapons."

"Those guards will probably kill us the minute we try to escape," Luke replied, "but we have no choice."

Fred the Red, who had brought the boys to the

amphitheater in the wagon, came over with a large cloth sack. He turned it upside down and dumped the contents on the dirt—shin guards, shoulder guards, a thick leather vest with a picture of a horse on it.

"Put these on, slaves," he ordered.

Then he handed each of the boys a helmet and a large square shield. The helmets were not like the bike or skateboard helmets you wear. They were big, heavy bronze helmets that some craftsman had clearly spent many days making. Luke's helmet was embossed with a picture of an ostrich. David's had a plumed peacock crest on it. The boys strapped on the armor and put the helmets on their heads.

"What about our swords?" Luke asked, casting a sideways glance at David.

"You will get a sword when you *need* a sword, Oceanus," said Fred the Red.

Outside the Palestra Grande, the crowd in the amphitheater could be heard. There must have been a lot of hoopla going on. People were laughing, booing, and roaring. It was like a pre-game tailgate party.

Crustus, the toothless pig thief they'd met in the wagon, saw the boys standing in the corner nervously. He limped over to them.

"Do not be apprehensive," he said. "Your battle will be over in five or ten minutes. They never last long. The citizens are impatient for what comes next. I wish you fine gentlemen good luck."

"Same to you," the boys said.

"To what gladiator school did you attend?" asked Crustus.

Luke and David looked at each other. There were *schools* for gladiators? Who knew?

"I went to Tiger Schulmann Karate Academy, in Boston, Massachusetts," Luke replied. Actually, Luke only took one karate class, when he was in first grade. Some kid hit him in the face and he ran out the door crying.

"I have never heard of such a place," Crustus said, and he walked away.

On the ground next to the wall was a line of stretchers. It was obvious who they were for—dead and dying gladiators.

The timer counted down: 81 minutes.

A man came over wearing a hat with wings on either side of it. His shoes also had wings on them, and he was carrying a staff with what looked like a snake wrapped around it. It appeared to be some kind of a costume.

"Gather around, gladiators," he announced. "I am Mercury the messenger god, the son of Jupiter. Today you will fight for the honor of Rome. In all probability, you will die. It is my job to escort your soul to the Underworld."

"Excuse me," David said, raising his hand. "May I ask a question?"

"No!" shouted the guy dressed as Mercury. "I have a few simple instructions you must follow. You were brought here to entertain the citizens of Pompeii and to please the gods. If you die too quickly, the crowd will not be entertained. The same is said if it takes you too *long* to die."

"So what you're saying is that we have to die in the right amount of time," David said sarcastically.

"That is correct," Mercury said. "You are here to put on a show. Hold your shield up to protect yourself from the blows. Engage the crowd. They like that. Try to get them on your side. And when you have lost and it is clear that your battle is futile, you must die with dignity. Remember, you will be dying for Rome. For the gods. You who are about to die, we honor you!"

"How about honoring us by letting us go free?" David suggested.

At that point, Fred the Red came over. He was

holding some papers.

"I will need all of you to sign this legal agreement and to swear the *sacramentum gladiatorium* oath."

All the prisoners who were in the wagon lined up to sign the paper. It was written in Latin.

"What does it say?" Luke asked. "I can't read."

"It says you agree to submit to beating, burning, and death by the sword if you do not perform as required," Fred the Red explained.

"And what happens if we don't sign?" asked Luke.

"Then you will be put to death instantly."

"So in other words," Luke said, "we're going to die if we sign, and we're going to die if we *don't* sign. So what's the difference?"

"The difference is that if you don't sign, you will be sacrificed to the gods," Fred the Red explained. "You will be stabbed one hundred times, and then your body will be dragged through the Gate of Death and hung upside down for the public's amusement until you are eaten by vultures. Of course, the choice is yours."

"Where do we sign?" asked Luke.

CHAPTER 12

SOME DIE SOONER THAN OTHERS

INSIDE THE AMPHITHEATER, IT LOOKED LIKE THE entire population of Pompeii had come out to see the gladiators fight. Every seat was taken, and some of the sections were standing room only.

The first four rows were filled with political and business leaders, senators, and knights. The bigwigs sat in a gilded box and stood out in their white, purple-bordered togas. Some of them had personal slaves holding umbrellas over their heads to shield them from the burning sun.

The rest of the crowd was separated by large stone tiers. Soldiers sat in a different section from civilians.

Married men sat in a different section from bachelors. Women and poor people got the worst seats, up in the twenty-first row. One thing that everyone shared was excitement and anticipation. Going to the gladiator games was not a daily or once-a-week event. This was a special occasion.

It should be remembered, reader, that there were no movies, TV, or internet to amuse the population in the year 79. *This* is what people did for fun. This was their entertainment.

Gladiator games always came with pageantry. There were no marching bands, of course. But men with long, curved horns played something that slightly resembled what we call music. Somebody played a water organ, which was a primitive instrument that worked by forcing air through pipes of different lengths. Guys came out banging big drums that were strapped to their waists. Jugglers roamed the stands.

These were the warm-up acts. Their job was to get the crowd in the mood for the main attraction. It was like the opening ceremonies of the Olympics.

"Glory to Rome!" announced a man holding a big megaphone. "Glory to Emperor Titus!"

"Glory to Emperor Titus!" the crowd shouted back.

The tenth emperor of Rome—Titus Vespasianus

Augustus—had only been in power for two months. So he wanted to win over the citizens of his empire. Loaves of bread and other goodies were tossed to the grateful masses. Perfumed water was sprayed on the sweaty crowd. For the children in attendance, little wooden balls called *missilia* were given out. Anything to keep the people happy—and the emperor in control.

That's why gladiator games were held in the first place, of course. They distracted the citizens from their everyday lives and gave them a way to blow off a little steam. The average Roman man may have led a hard life, but watching two *other* guys fight to the death made him forget about his own problems, at least for a little while.

Vendors walked through the crowd selling food and wine. Children played with gladiator action figures made of clay. People waited patiently under the hot sun. But the crowd was starting to get restless. They wanted more than "pomp and circumstance." They wanted blood.

In the Palestra Grande next door, the gladiators looked away when Fred the Red approached. Nobody wanted to make eye contact with him. Nobody wanted to be chosen to go first.

"I'm starved," David said to Luke. "I wonder if they're going to feed us anything."

"You should have had a few of those dormice when they offered them to you," Luke replied. "That stuff was *good*."

Fred the Red walked directly over to Crustus, the limping, toothless pig thief.

"You're up first," Fred the Red said simply. "Get ready."

There was a look of resignation on Crustus's face. He closed his eyes for a moment to say a silent prayer. Two guards took him by the elbows to escort him to a stone archway with an iron gate that separated the Palestra Grande from the amphitheater. Before the guards could take him away, Luke and David went over to him.

"Good-bye, Crustus," David said, putting his hand on the man's shoulder. "Good luck."

"I will need it," Crustus replied.

A hush came over the crowd.

"Citizens and free men of Pompeii," bellowed the announcer through his megaphone. "Welcome to the most spectacular gladiator games ever to be presented, thanks to your great emperor Titus."

The crowd roared in approval.

"Our first competitors," hollered the announcer, "are Julianus the slave of Herculaneum . . . and Crustus the criminal pig thief!"

The crowd roared again.

"They will fight to the death. What shall be their fate?"

"Death!" chanted the crowd. "Death! Death! Death!"

One of the guards handed Crustus a sword and gave him a shove toward the iron gate. Two other guards pulled ropes on either side of the gate to slowly lift it up. Crustus walked through the stone archway. The gate was lowered behind him. There was another roar from the crowd as he stepped into the arena, and yet another one when his opponent entered the arena from an archway on the far side of the amphitheater.

Luke, David, and some other gladiators edged forward to try to see the action through the bars, but the guards pushed them back. David didn't really want to watch anyway. He never liked the sight of blood.

"I don't know how to fight," David whispered to Luke. "What about you? Have you ever been in a real fight?"

"No, but I've seen a million martial arts movies," Luke replied. "And when I was little, me and my friends used to have pretend fights in the backyard. We used sticks as swords and garbage can covers as shields."

"Me and my friends fought with light sabers," David said.

Luke and David couldn't see the action going on inside the arena. But they could hear it—the slash of one metal sword hitting another one, over and over again. The grunting and the cries of pain. People in the audience screaming and cheering.

"Fight boldly for your life, Crustus!" a voice in the crowd hollered.

With each clanging blow, David cringed. He could only imagine what was happening inside the arena. He knew his turn might be next.

After a few short minutes, a gasp was heard, a roar, and then silence. The fight was over. The crowd clapped in approval. The musicians started playing again. David rushed over to Fred the Red, who appeared to be in charge of all the gladiators.

"What happened to Crustus?" he asked.

"He is dead," said Fred the Red. "Next!"

David sank to his knees.

"He was a good man," he moaned.

"What makes you think he was a good man?" asked Fred the Red. "He stole another man's pig."

"But he was *hungry*," David said.

"Hunger is not a justification for stealing," explained Fred the Red. "The deviant criminal must be punished to show the citizens what happens when one breaks the laws of the land. There is no other way to sustain law and order."

"Is it fair to die just for stealing a pig?" asked David.

"We will all die one day," Fred the Red explained. "Some die sooner than others. That is the only difference. It pleases the gods."

There was no point in having a philosophical discussion about right and wrong with Fred the Red. David sneaked a peek at the timer. There were 69 minutes left. A little more than an hour. He ran over to Luke, who was off to the side, stretching his legs as if he was getting ready for a track meet.

"Crustus is dead," David told his friend. "We're doomed, dude! We don't know how to fight. Either we're gonna die out there or the mountain's gonna blow and—"

"Oceanus!" shouted Fred the Red.

All eyes turned toward Luke.

"What do you want?" the boy asked.

"What do you *think* I want?" hollered Fred the Red. "It is your turn to fight!"

CHAPTER 13

THE ELEMENT OF SURPRISE

UP UNTIL THIS MOMENT, LUKE HAD BEEN PRETTY much holding it together. He had been hoping that with so many available gladiators, maybe his name wouldn't get called. Maybe he would be able to find a way out of this situation without having to fight for his life.

"Come with me, Oceanus," said Fred the Red.

"I don't *want* to die!" Luke howled, backing away. "I didn't do anything wrong! I don't even know why I'm here!"

"Are you a coward?" Fred the Red asked, grabbing Luke by the arm. "Honor Emperor Titus and die like a man!"

"I'm not a man!" Luke shrieked, pulling away. "I'm just a kid!"

Fred the Red called two guards over. They grabbed Luke roughly while the boy struggled to get free of their grasp.

"You are strong," Fred the Red told Luke. "You would be wise to save your strength. If you put up as much fight in the arena as you are putting up now, you will do fine. Let's go! The citizens are impatient!"

Luke stopped resisting, and the guards loosened their grip on him. David came over and wrapped his arms around Luke. Tears filled their eyes.

"I love you, man," David whispered.

"I love you, too," Luke replied. "You are my brother from another mother. If some miracle happens and I survive this, I'll meet you and the girls at the meeting spot."

"I'll see you there," David said, trying his best to be positive.

Luke adjusted his body armor and picked up his shield.

"Here, take your sword," said Fred the Red.

The word *gladiator* comes from *gladius*, which is the Latin word for sword. Most people don't know this, but there were different kinds of weapons for different kinds of gladiators. The Romans liked to mix things up to keep the crowd interested.

The *dimachaerus* gladiators fought with two swords, one in each hand. The *equites* gladiators entered the arena on horseback. The *essedarii* battled from chariots. Luke was a *thrax* gladiator. He was given a curved short sword and a small square shield.

Fred the Red led Luke to the big iron gate under the archway leading into the arena.

"May fortune smile upon you, Oceanus," he told Luke. "Perhaps the gods will favor you, and you will live to fight another day."

Luke said nothing. There was nothing to say. He took a deep breath and gripped his sword tightly. The gate was pulled open. Any thought of making a run for it was gone. There was no place to run.

A huge cheer rang out when Luke stepped into the arena. The gate was lowered behind him with a heavy clang. He was alone out there.

"Our next gladiator," announced the guy with the megaphone, "battling for his first time in Pompeii . . . is the slave . . . Oceanus!"

Luke turned around 360 degrees as the citizens applauded and stamped their feet for him. The arena itself was a large oval, smaller than a football field, but larger than a basketball court. On the walls of the arena were paintings of gladiators in combat. The ground was sandy dirt. Luke could see patches of blood and smell the rotting flesh of previous competitors.

This wasn't all that different from a ballgame at Fenway Park in Boston, it occurred to Luke. It wasn't that different from *any* modern sporting event, really. But instead of watching two teams compete to score the most runs, goals, or points, the crowd would watch two men try to kill each other. And instead of winning money or trophies, the victor was allowed to live—if he was lucky.

"He's just a boy!" shouted a voice from the crowd.

Oh, good, Luke said to himself, *maybe they'll change their minds and let me go.*

"Kill the boy!" shouted another voice.

"Are you going to fight like a man?" somebody else hollered.

Luke looked up at the crowd. It was like a circus. The Roman Empire wasn't at war, so these fake gladiator wars were staged to amuse the population. People had brought their *children* with them. Kids were chanting, taunting, eating, and laughing. They had seen blood. Now they wanted to see more. It was disgusting.

These people are sick, Luke muttered to himself. Sweat was pouring off him. He wiped his forehead with his sleeve.

At the other end of the arena was another archway with an iron gate in front of it, where his opponent was about to emerge. The applause had to die down before the gate would be lifted, to build anticipation.

"Our next gladiator," the guy with the megaphone finally announced, "all the way from Rome, is the criminal Vulcan, who committed the crime of criticizing Emperor Titus!"

"Boooooo!" the crowd shouted as the gate went up. *"Boooooo!"*

"I get it," Luke muttered to himself. "It's just like professional wrestling. We each play a character. He's the heel and I'm the babyface."

The gladiator named Vulcan came out. He was a big, ugly, bald guy, maybe 250 pounds. He had an arrogant scowl on his face, big muscles on his arms and legs, and scars from previous battles on his stomach. Luke cringed.

That guy looks like he takes steroids, he thought.

In the stands, money was changing hands. People

were making bets on which gladiator would live and which would die.

Vulcan lumbered out to the center of the arena. Luke's instinct was to run away, but he decided the only way to beat the big guy would be to use his wits. He walked out to meet Vulcan in the middle and put out his hand to shake. The big guy ignored it.

"This is all fake, right?" Luke asked Vulcan when they were face-to-face. "We don't really go at it, do we?"

"Grrrr," replied Vulcan. He shoved Luke with his shield, pushing the boy backward.

"Maybe you and I can work out a little deal," Luke suggested. "I'll hit you a few times. You hit me a few times. One of us falls down . . ."

"Grrrr . . ."

Vulcan shoved him again, harder this time. Luke stumbled and fell backward. He was sitting in the dirt.

Okay, this is real, he said to himself. Vulcan looked angry. It wasn't clear if he even spoke a language.

"Fight! Fight! Fight!" the bloodthirsty crowd chanted as one.

Luke stood up.

"And what if I refuse?" he shouted, throwing down his sword.

"Boooooo!" the crowd shouted.

"The boy is too timid to fight!" somebody yelled. "He is a coward!"

"Why are you reluctant to die?" yelled somebody else. "The gods will honor you."

"Die with honor, Oceanus!"

"Coward! Coward! Coward!"

"Sacrifice the boy to the gods!"

The iron gate at the far end of the arena opened again. Another man came out dressed as Mars, the Roman god of war. He was carrying a long iron stick. It was the length of a sword, but it wasn't sharp. The tip was glowing bright red-orange, as it had just been taken out of a fire.

"Those who lack the enthusiasm to fight must be persuaded!" shouted Mars. The crowd cheered.

"Burn him!" somebody shouted as Mars advanced toward Luke with the red-hot poker.

"Okay, okay!" Luke said, picking up his sword. "I'll fight."

The crowd cheered. *This* is what they had come to see. Mars retreated, and went back to where he came from.

Luke and Vulcan circled each other slowly in the middle of the arena, sizing each other up, swords at the ready, looking for an opening. Luke tried to remember all those martial arts movies he had seen.

"Oceanus! Oceanus! Oceanus!"

Vulcan charged forward like a boar and took a wild swing with his sword, but Luke dodged sideways and scampered out of the way. Luke lunged with his sword, but Vulcan blocked it with his shield.

"Vulcan! Vulcan! Vulcan!"

Luke didn't have any real fighting experience, but he could see that Vulcan was slow and clumsy. Luke could run around him, using his speed to confuse and torment the big man. He remembered reading how Muhammad Ali did exactly that to win the heavyweight championship as a young man.

Vulcan flailed at Luke again, and only the boy's lightning-fast reaction time prevented a serious injury as the sword whistled inches from his ear. Luke launched a counterattack, slashing back, and his sword clanged against Vulcan's sword as it was pushed out of the way.

They went back and forth like that with a flurry of overhand blows. The crowd was on its feet and cheering, but Luke barely heard it. He was in the moment. He had forgotten all about Mount Vesuvius erupting. Right now, the only thing that mattered was protecting his vital organs.

The sword was starting to feel heavy. Luke had to swing it with two hands like a baseball bat, sometimes hitting Vulcan's shield and sometimes hitting his armor. He knew that if he didn't do some damage fast, he was going to lose. Every time a blow landed, there was the sound of a trumpet blast from the musicians who had been entertaining the crowd.

But even as he tired, Luke was gaining confidence. It didn't seem possible for him to stand toe-to-toe with a man the size of Vulcan. But in a life-or-death situation, we call up a hidden reserve of untapped strength. There are stories of women who have picked up a car when their baby was trapped underneath it. It's like having temporary superpowers.

"Oceanus! Oceanus! Oceanus!"

It actually looked like Luke was winning as he traded blows with the bigger man. He stood firm as he planted his leg and lunged at Vulcan the way he had seen it done in countless movies. But that's when he made a crucial mistake. He got a little too close, and Vulcan's sword nicked him on the arm. Luke looked down and saw blood.

"Owww!" he shouted.

Vulcan pounced. He charged toward Luke, ramming

his shield against the side of the boy's head and denting his helmet. Luke's ears were ringing. Caught off balance, his knees buckled and he stumbled, landing on his back. When he hit the ground, he lost the grip on his shield. Vulcan thundered forward, standing over Luke, his sword poised to plunge into the boy's exposed throat. It was a desperate situation.

The crowd roared in approval. They were on their feet now.

"Vulcan! Vulcan! Vulcan!"

For a gladiator who was about to be killed, the proper etiquette was to beg for mercy by dropping his sword and raising one finger. The victor could then choose to back off or—more commonly—kill his opponent and put him out of his misery.

But Luke didn't know anything about gladiator etiquette. He just knew he had no shield and Vulcan was about to slice him open.

The crowd was going crazy, screaming, waving handkerchiefs, and making thumbs-up or thumbs-down signs to indicate what Vulcan should do to Luke.

"Iugula!" shouted half the crowd. "Kill him!"

"Mitte!" shouted the other half. "Let him go!"

"Grrrr . . ."

* * *

By all rights, reader, this is where the story of the Flashback Four must come to an end. The timer counted down: 59 minutes. Less than an hour left. But that didn't matter. Luke was about to be killed. The rest of the team was in captivity and sure to be wiped out along with the rest of Pompeii.

But you've probably noticed there are quite a few pages left in this book. So let's continue.

Luke was on the ground, on his back, with Vulcan looming over him and poised to plunge his sword into the boy's carotid artery. Luke had only one option, and it was the oldest trick in the book. Fortunately, the book hadn't been written yet.

"Behind you!" he shouted at Vulcan, pointing over the big man's head. "Watch out!"

The element of surprise. It's a marvelous weapon.

When Vulcan turned around to see what was behind him, Luke jumped to his feet and swung his sword as hard as he could. Vulcan saw a blur of movement from the corner of his eye, but he couldn't react in time. Luke's sword caught the big man flush on the side of his helmet. Vulcan was knocked sideways, staggered, and went sprawling facedown in the dirt. His helmet went flying. Vulcan was still. It looked like he was unconscious.

The crowd went crazy. They had never seen such an audacious move before.

"Oceanus! Oceanus! Oceanus!"

Luke bent over and put his hands on his knees, trying to catch his breath. He turned to look at Vulcan, who was not moving.

"Is Vulcan dead?" shouted the announcer through his megaphone. "Or is he a faker? Let us find out for sure."

The guy dressed as Mars came out again with his red-hot poker. He touched it to Vulcan's back. The big man twitched and screamed in pain.

"Vulcan is not yet dead!" shouted the announcer. That riled up the crowd even more.

"Finish him off, Oceanus!"

"Iugula! Iugula! Iugula!" chanted the crowd.

Luke looked at Vulcan on the ground. Then he shook his head and flipped his sword up in the air the way baseball players flip their bats.

"Boooooo!"

"Why is Oceanus reluctant to kill?" somebody shouted.

"Boooooo!"

"You people are sick," Luke yelled, but nobody

could hear him over the noise.

He staggered back to the gate, where Fred the Red was waiting.

"You fought bravely," he told Luke. "You put on a good show and pleased the citizens. More than that, you pleased the gods."

Fred the Red placed a laurel crown of victory on Luke's head and handed him a palm branch.

"That's *it*?" asked Luke. "For winning I get a piece of a *tree*? Am I at least free to go now?"

"Free to go?" Fred the Red said with a laugh. "If you continue to fight bravely for three years, and then, if the gods have mercy, you may be freed. *May.*"

MEANWHILE, BACK IN BOSTON . . .

MISS Z AND MRS. VADER HAD NO IDEA WHAT WAS happening in Pompeii. They had been going about their morning, making phone calls, answering emails, drinking coffee, and doing all those other routine things that grown-ups do.

Miss Z spent some time on the phone with a real estate developer who had expressed interest in her idea, which now had a name—the Museum of Historic Photography, or MOHP. Washington, DC, seemed to be the perfect location for the museum, a block from the National Air and Space Museum.

"Yes, I'll have photos of historic events that have

never been seen before," she said excitedly into the phone. "You're going to be amazed."

With the photo of the *Titanic* up on her wall, Miss Z had renewed enthusiasm for her museum. In an hour, the Flashback Four would be delivering another photo for the collection—Mount Vesuvius blowing its top in the year 79. Miss Z could barely contain her excitement. She was already brainstorming about other historic photos she could get—Washington crossing the Delaware. America's Founding Fathers signing the Declaration of Independence. Leonardo da Vinci painting the *Mona Lisa*. The possibilities were endless. She could send the Flashback Four back to prehistoric times to take the first and only photograph of a living dinosaur!

Mrs. Vader glanced at her watch. It was 11:20 in Pompeii time. The kids had left for Pompeii at exactly 10:15. They had two hours to scope out the town, find a location, and take the photo of the mountain exploding at noon. At 12:15, it would be time to bring them back home. Plenty of time.

"Do you think we should send a text to Isabel to see how the kids are doing?" Mrs. Vader asked her boss.

"I don't want to pester them too much," Miss Z replied. "You know the way children are. Leave them be. Isabel is a big girl. She'll get in touch if they need us."

Mrs. Vader let some time go by, but she couldn't stop thinking about the Flashback Four. It seemed like it had been quite a while since Isabel had reported in. Mrs. Vader checked the computer. The last communication from Isabel had been **EVERYTHING GOING SMOOTHLY. LOOKING FOR PERFECT PHOTO LOCATION.**

She resolved to stop worrying. She checked to see if the mail had arrived, and paid a few bills. When those tasks were completed, there was nothing else that needed to be done.

"I really think we should text the kids," she told Miss Z.

"Okay, okay," Miss Z replied. "If you say so. Go ahead."

EVERYTHING STILL GOING SMOOTHLY? Mrs. Vader typed.

She watched the screen to read the response when it came back.

There was no response.

"Isabel usually replies right away," Mrs. Vader said a little nervously.

"Be patient," Miss Z told her. "I'm sure she'll text back in a few seconds."

A few seconds passed. There was no reply.

"They must be busy," Miss Z said. "Give it a few minutes and then try again."

Mrs. Vader went to the other side of the office to replace the filter in the coffee machine. That killed a few minutes. Then she came back to the computer.

YOU KIDS OK? she texted.

Nothing. No response. Now *both* of them were getting nervous.

"This isn't like Isabel," Miss Z said.

"Maybe the TTT is broken," Mrs. Vader guessed.

"It's worked like a charm up until now," replied Miss Z. "Try again."

Mrs. Vader typed *another* text.

ISABEL?

As you know, reader, this entire effort was useless. They could try a *million* times and the result would be the same. The TTT had been snatched away from Isabel and crushed after the Flashback Four were grabbed on the street in Pompeii. But Miss Z and Mrs. Vader didn't know that.

"Something must have gone wrong," Miss Z said, in the understatement of the year.

Silently, she imagined all the things that could have

happened. The kids might have lost the TTT. Maybe they dropped it in water again and it was ruined. Or the extreme heat of Pompeii had caused the battery to drain. Maybe they had been pickpocketed again. *Anything* could have happened.

It did *not* cross Miss Z's mind that maybe the Flashback Four had been forced into slavery and Isabel and Julia were chained to a wall in a Pompeii dungeon while Luke and David were being forced to fight for their lives as gladiators.

Mrs. Vader checked the time again. It was eleven thirty in Pompeii. The scheduled pickup time was twelve fifteen, forty-five minutes away.

"Maybe we should think about picking them up early," Mrs. Vader suggested.

Miss Z closed her eyes. It helped her think.

If she brought the Flashback Four home early, it would certainly remove them from a possibly dangerous situation. But that would only work if the kids were at the meeting spot at that moment. She didn't know where they were. There was no way to find out. And it was unlikely that they were at the meeting spot, because they would have been out exploring the town.

Furthermore, what if somebody *else* happened to be standing at the meeting spot? If she fired up the

Board to bring the kids back, she would bring back whoever happened to be standing at that spot at that moment. She had already made that mistake once with that Thomas Maloney guy from the *Titanic*.

To make things *more* complicated, if she activated the Board and accidentally brought back somebody else instead of the Flashback Four, she wouldn't be able to try again. The technology of the Board was very advanced, but it only allowed her to do an upload once to a specific place and time. If she messed up for any reason, there would be no second chance. No do-overs. The kids would then be stuck in Pompeii for the rest of their lives.

And the rest of their lives would last less than an hour, when they would be incinerated by the volcano.

Finally, needless to say, if she messed up, Miss Z could forget about getting that photo of Mount Vesuvius blowing its top.

She rubbed her forehead and shook her head. *Why does this always happen?* she wondered. She had worked so hard and spent so much money to perfect this technology. She had been so careful to get the right clothes for the kids, and to prepare them for every possibility they might encounter on their mission. It was supposed to be so *easy*. In and out.

Take the picture and come home. Why did something always go wrong?

"Bringing them back early is too risky," she finally said to Mrs. Vader. "Let's stick with the original plan. Unless we hear from them, we'll bring them back as scheduled, at twelve fifteen."

CHAPTER 15

NEXT VICTIM

IN POMPEII, LUKE STAGGERED BACK TO THE PALEStra Grande after his unexpected victory over Vulcan. He was sweating, exhausted, and slightly wounded, with a trickle of blood dripping down his arm. But he was still on his feet, and the truth is, he was feeling somewhat exhilarated. How could he *not* be? The cheering from the bloodthirsty crowd was still ringing in his ears.

"Oceanus! Oceanus! Oceanus!"

Luke could hardly believe he had defeated a man so much bigger and stronger.

"You're alive!" David yelled, running over to hug

his friend. "I can't believe you survived!"

"It wasn't easy," Luke told him as he gingerly sat down on the dirt against the stone wall.

"You're a mess, dude," David said.

"You should see the other guy," Luke replied, wiping some blood off his arm.

"Is he dead?"

"No," Luke said, a little defensively. "Are you crazy? Do you think I could kill a man? They were booing me because I *didn't* kill him. I did whack the guy pretty good, though. Knocked him out. And you know what I did after that?"

"What?"

"I did a bat flip with the sword," Luke said, trying not to laugh.

"You are *kidding* me."

For readers who don't understand the point of a bat flip, a short explanation—after baseball players hit a home run, sometimes they will flip their bat in the air as a gesture of triumph. The opposing team, and especially the pitcher, view it as a provocative gesture. And it is. The batter is sort of sticking it in the face of the pitcher.

"Those nuts in the crowd were freaking out," Luke said. "They never saw anything like *that* before."

David looked at the timer. There were 34 minutes left.

"Listen, we need to get out of here," he said. "We're running out of time."

"Can I just sit here for a minute?" Luke asked. "I'm wiped out."

While Luke rested, David looked around for a way out of the Palestra Grande. There was no roof over it. Just a low wall on all four sides. A couple of guards were hanging around near the gates, but they didn't look like they were paying close attention.

"I think we might be able to climb that wall," David said, gesturing toward a corner where a statue was positioned a few feet away from the edge.

"You think so?" Luke asked, not all that excited about the thought of another physical challenge.

"We've got to try," David said. "Otherwise we're just stuck here when Vesuvius erupts. "Come on, I'll help you up, and then you pull me up."

"Okay," Luke said wearily as he struggled to his feet.

They casually strolled over to the corner, doing their best to avoid attracting any attention to themselves. David quickly clasped his hands together to create a step so Luke could hoist himself up on the bottom of the statue. Luke planted his foot on it. Then he pulled himself up so he was standing on the statue's pedestal.

"Good," David said. "Now, quick, pull me up."

That's when Fred the Red came running over, with two guards holding long spears.

"Oceanus! Hilarius!" he shouted. "Where do you think *you're* going?"

"We're, uh . . . just exercising," Luke explained lamely as he jumped down from the pedestal. "We need to work on our quads."

Fred the Red wasn't buying it.

"Hilarius!" he shouted. "Come with me! *Now*!"

"Why? What did I do?"

"Nothing yet," said Fred the Red. "You are next."

"Next?" David asked, backing away. "Next for *what*?"

"What do you think, stupid slave?" Fred the Red said, slapping him. "Next to fight! Get your helmet! The citizens are waiting for their entertainment."

"W-what?!" David stammered. "B-but I never . . . I don't know how to fight."

"Guards!" Fred the Red shouted. "Help Hilarius get ready for battle."

As the guards seized David by the arms, Luke

pleaded on behalf of his friend.

"Can't you pick one of the other guys?" Luke asked. "He'll get killed out there!"

"So?" Fred the Red said. "That is not my concern. Guards, take Hilarius away!"

Luke begged for just one minute alone with his friend, and Fred the Red granted it.

"Listen to me," Luke whispered to David. "I know a trick. It worked for me. It will work for you too."

"Yeah? What?"

"Get the guy close to you, close enough to look in his eyes," Luke said. "Then, act really terrified, point over his head, and shout, 'Look out behind you!' When he turns around to see what's behind him, smack him as hard as you can on the side of his head with your sword. He won't know what hit him."

"That actually worked?" David asked, disbelieving. "That's the oldest trick in the book."

"It's the year 79," Luke replied. "They don't have books."

"Okay, I'll try it," David said as the guards grabbed him by the arms again.

"Here is your weapon, Hilarius," said Fred the Red as he handed David a long spear with three short prongs at the end. It looked like an oversized fork. In later centuries, it would be called a trident.

David looked at it with disbelief.

"Are you joking?" he asked. "What am I supposed to do with this thing? Catch a fish?"

"It is a very dangerous weapon," Fred the Red assured him. "It is the weapon of Neptune, the god of the sea."

"It looks like a toy," David complained. "How come Luke got a regular sword and I have to use this thing?"

"It is not your only weapon," Fred the Red said as one of the guards handed him a cloth bag. "You will have something else as well."

He reached into the bag and pulled out a large net made from thick rope.

"Really?" David asked. "You're giving me a *net*? Am I going to be playing volleyball out there? You're putting me on, right?"

But it was no joke. Just as some gladiators fought with two long swords and some fought with one curved short sword, others were given a trident and a net. As I mentioned earlier, the Romans liked to mix things up to keep the crowd interested.

David wasn't happy, obviously.

"That's *it*?" he asked. "All I get is a weird-looking fork and a net? I need a hand grenade, or a bazooka, or something. Don't I at least get a shield?"

"You are a net-man!" Fred the Red told him, as if that explained it all.

"This is it," David mumbled, shaking his head. "I'm gonna die."

But he had no choice. David put on his helmet and picked up the trident and net. Fred the Red led him to the same gate where Luke had entered the arena. David waited for the gate to be pulled up and his name to be announced. He was trembling with fear. Luke broke away from the guard who was holding him and ran over to his friend.

"You can *do* this, David!" Luke said. "I survived. So can you."

"I'm scared, man."

"Look, the other guy is gonna have the same weapons you do," Luke told him. "So it will be a fair fight. Remember what I told you. Use the *look-behind-you* trick. It'll work. Good luck."

"What if I don't make it?" David asked. "What if the guy is twice my size?"

"Keep telling yourself that he's just a man," Luke said, his hand on David's shoulder. "He gets up in the morning and puts his pants on one leg at a time, just like you do."

"Just a man," repeated David, closing his eyes. "Just a man."

"Good. Now go get him!"

"Our next gladiator," announced the guy with the megaphone, "another slave battling for the first time in Pompeii, is the one, the only . . . Hilarius!"

The gate was raised slowly. David stepped out into the light and the gate lowered behind him. The crowd erupted into cheers. The people of Pompeii had rarely seen a gladiator with dark skin. The novelty was fascinating to them.

"Hilarius! Hilarius! Hilarius!"

"My name is David!" shouted David.

He stood there and looked all around the arena, just as Luke had when he was introduced. Then he peered at the gate on the other side to see who would emerge from that end.

"And now . . . his opponent," announced the guy with the megaphone, "all the way from Naples . . . is the brave, the strong . . . They call him . . . Panthera!"

The gate was slowly lifted up. And out of the gate walked . . .

A tiger.

"Oh, shoot!" David shouted.

CHAPTER 16

WHAT AM I SUPPOSED TO DO *NOW*?

YES, IT WAS A TIGER. *PANTHERA TIGRIS*, IF YOU want to get technical about it.

Just like human life during the Roman Empire, animal lives were cheap. Teams of hunters were sent all over Europe, Asia, and Africa with instructions to bring back deer, bears, lions, tigers, and leopards, as well as more unusual animals to excite the crowd— elephants, rhinos, giraffes, ostriches, and crocodiles. Sometimes the animals would be sacrificed in hopes of pleasing the gods. And sometimes they became part of the gladiator shows, either fighting against other animals or against people. Gladiators who fought animals were called *venatores*.

"Hilarius! Hilarius! Hilarius!" chanted the crowd.

David just stood there in front of the iron gate for a moment, stunned. He had assumed his opponent would be some kind of a beast, but he wasn't expecting a *real* beast. The crowd roared in approval when the tiger entered the arena.

"He's just a *man*, eh?" David asked angrily without turning around to face Luke, who was a few feet behind him on the other side of the gate.

"I'm sorry, dude," Luke said.

"He puts his pants on one leg at a time, eh?" David asked.

"Really sorry."

"He'll have the same weapons as I do, eh?" David asked.

"Seriously, man. I'm so sorry."

"I guess he won't be falling for the old *look-behind-you* trick, will he?" David asked.

The tiger slinked around, sniffing the ground. It didn't seem to notice there was a gladiator on the other side of the arena.

"How come *you* got to fight a plain old *guy*," he

shouted behind him at Luke, "and I have to fight a *tiger*?"

"I'm so sorry, dude," Luke replied. "I had no idea."

"What am I supposed to do *now*?" David asked.

"Try to fend him off with that fork thing," Luke suggested. "Keep his teeth and claws away from you."

"Gee, that's a big help," David mumbled. "I'm gonna *die* here."

"Look at it this way," said Luke, who was always trying to look on the bright side. "You have a weapon, and he doesn't. So you have an advantage."

"Yeah, but he has an advantage too," David replied. "He's a *tiger*!"

The walls around the arena were seven feet high. David turned around and tried to climb the gate.

"Let me back in!" he shouted through the bars. "Please! I'll do anything!"

"Get *down*, slave!" shouted the guards, poking their spears through the holes in the gate.

David fell back down to the dirt. The crowd roared with laughter.

Interestingly, when he was in third grade, David's class had done a unit about endangered species. And quite

185

coincidentally, David's topic for his report had been tigers. He tried to remember what he had written. . . .

Tigers: Friend or Foe?
By David Williams, grade 3

I love animals, and especially tigers, because tigers are cool! They are striped land animals and they are the largest of all the cat species. A tiger can weigh more than eight hundred pounds. Wow, that's heavy. I wouldn't want one of them to sit on me! They can run really fast, too, like thirty or forty miles an hour. And they can jump more than thirty feet. Tigers also live a long time. More than twenty-five years! They are the national animal of Bangladesh, India, Malaysia, and South Korea.

I wouldn't want to get into a fight with a tiger. They are carnivores. That means they eat meat. Tigers don't usually eat humans, but sometimes they do. In fact, tigers cause more human deaths than any other wild mammal. When tigers attack a human or another animal, they usually go for the throat. They will grab onto the neck of their prey. Then they break the spinal cord. Then they pierce the windpipe. Then they sever the jugular vein. The prey dies from strangulation.

"Oh, shoot!" David shouted again.

The tiger looked a little confused after it entered the arena. It was startled by the sound of the crowd. It had grown up in the jungle and spent the last few weeks locked in a small cage. This was a new environment for it.

David stood in one place like a statue, out of fear and common sense. He was trying to make himself invisible. Maybe the tiger wouldn't notice him and just leave him alone.

The tiger, more than anything else, was hungry. It hadn't been fed in a few days. This was on purpose. The animals that were pitted against gladiators needed a little extra motivation to fight, so they were kept hungry. Human beings were not part of their regular diet.

The tiger stalked around slowly, looking left and right, sniffing the ground for something to eat. Unfortunately, the only edible thing in the arena was David.

"Hilarius! Hilarius! Hilarius!"

"Fight, slave!" a man shouted at David. "Or are you a coward?"

Somebody threw a rock, and it landed in the

middle of the arena. The tiger saw it hit the ground out the corner of its eye and looked up. That's when it noticed David, standing stiffly about fifty yards away. Slowly and cautiously, the tiger started moving along the wall in David's direction.

"I'm going to die. I'm going to die. I'm going to die," David mumbled to himself.

He realized he wasn't going to win this battle by becoming invisible. He started walking backward along the wall. But he would have to come up with another strategy. The tiger was moving faster than he was, and getting closer.

Stay calm, David thought. *It's just a big cat, right? I used to have a cat, but we had to give it away because my mom was allergic to it. I love cats. Cats are cute and cuddly—*

That's when the tiger opened its mouth and let out a roar. They could hear it echo up in the top level of the amphitheater.

"Oh, shoot!" David shouted again.

The crowd gasped.

The tiger charged toward David.

He dropped the trident and the net and ran for his life.

The tiger was gaining ground on him.

Well, this is *surely* where the story of the Flashback Four ends, right? David is going to get eaten by the tiger while Luke, Isabel, and Julia will be stuck in Pompeii and have their all-too-brief lives ended when the volcano erupts and destroys everything in sight.

What a sad and tragic ending, especially in a book for *children*. Your innocent eyes and ears probably wouldn't be able to handle such a depressing and violent ending like that. Children's books are supposed to end happily, with the main characters looking ahead to their bright future and further adventures. Maybe the author—not me—is going to come up with some miraculous way to get the Flashback Four out of this predicament. But he'd better do it fast, because there are only 27 minutes left on the timer, and only a few more chapters left in this book.

From his years of playing basketball and baseball, David was in good shape. And he was fast, one of the fastest kids in his school. He took off, hugging the wall as he ran around the perimeter of the oval arena. The tiger was right behind him. The crowd was loving it, screaming and laughing at the spectacle. To them, Hilarius was hilarious.

While tigers may be able to run forty miles per hour and the fastest human can only run about twenty-three miles per hour, this was *not* a particularly fast tiger. He was old, more than twenty years. That was why it was possible for the Romans to capture him in the first place.

David was able to stay about five steps in front of the tiger all the way around the arena. In the middle of their second lap, though, both of them were start-ing to slow down. David was getting winded. So was the tiger. But it was relentless. It kept moving toward David, snarling and growling. It was hungry, and there was food right in front of it.

As he completed a second lap around the arena, David saw the trident and net on the ground in front of him. He rushed to scoop them up.

"Fight, coward!" somebody shouted from the crowd. "Fight for your honor, and the honor of Rome!"

The tiger kept advancing on David.

He kept walking backward. As an animal lover, he didn't want to use the sharp edge of the trident. But he would do whatever he had to do to survive.

David started opening the net. It was bigger than he'd originally thought. Fully opened, it was about as large as a king-size bed.

The tiger opened its mouth and roared. It had two razor-sharp teeth, perfect for cutting into flesh. David held the net up, still keeping one hand on the trident.

The tiger wasn't dumb. It knew it couldn't catch David by running. The boy was too fast. Its best chance would be to gather up its remaining energy and attack with a bold leap at David's throat.

So that's what it did. One last roar, and then it was all teeth and flying claws. The crowd gasped.

David instinctively threw up the net so it was between him and the tiger. He stepped to the side like a bullfighter. Or, in his case, like a batter who gets out of the way of a fastball coming at his head.

The tiger hit the middle of the net with its face and tumbled to the ground, rolling over so the net fell on top of it. Thinking quickly, David ran over and grabbed the edges of the net to wrap it around the struggling animal.

"Hilarius! Hilarius! Hilarius!"

The tiger was tangled up inside the net. It struggled to get free for a minute, but only ensnared itself more tightly in rope. It realized its situation was hopeless. It stopped fighting.

The tiger was out of breath, panting. So was David.

"Stab it!" somebody yelled. And then the crowd started to chant.

"Stab it! Stab it! Stab it!"

David looked up at the crowd disgustedly.

"No!" he shouted.

"Boooooooo!"

Food and garbage rained down into the arena. The people came to see gladiators and animals killed, not captured.

"You people are *worse* than animals!" David shouted at them. "Tigers are an endangered species!"

He was about to walk toward the gate, but then he remembered that after Luke had won *his* fight, he'd ended it with a triumphant bat flip. So David flipped the trident up in the air and defiantly walked toward the gate.

The trident went about ten feet up in the air.

Then it came down.

And it landed in the one place David didn't want it to land.

In the tiger.

The tiger let out a tortured roar. So did the crowd.

Hearing the noise, David turned around. He saw

the trident sticking into the tiger's belly. It was gasping for breath as its front and rear paws flailed around.

"Nooooo!" David shouted, falling to his knees in horror.

The tiger was dead.

WORKING GIRLS

WHEN WE LAST SAW ISABEL AND JULIA, THEY were chained to opposite walls of a dark, dank, dangerous dungeon, their situation hopeless. The girls were tired and hungry. Their ankles and wrists were sore from the chains that bound them. Both of them had been crying.

"What do you think the boys are doing right now?" Isabel asked.

The girls, of course, had no idea that David and Luke were in the amphitheater, fighting for their lives.

"Oh, they're probably lounging around some

Roman bathhouse with girls in bikinis feeding them grapes," said Julia. "Isn't that what men did all the time during the Roman Empire?"

"You've seen too many movies," Isabel told her. "I don't think the Romans even *had* bikinis."

Isabel was right. The bikini wasn't invented until 1946, by Frenchman Louis Réard. He named it after a group of islands in the Pacific, where the United States was conducting nuclear tests. But that's another story for another day.

It was almost eleven o'clock. Mount Vesuvius was going to blow in an hour. But the girls didn't know the time, because David had the timer. Julia and Isabel were dozing on and off when the dungeon door opened with a loud screech. Startled, they looked up. A woman had entered their cell.

"Slaves!" she shouted as she went to unlock Julia's chains. "Come with me!"

"Well, it's about time!" Julia said as her ankles were freed. "Those things are cutting into my skin."

"You've got to listen to us!" Isabel told the woman. "Vesuvius is going to erupt. It's going to destroy Pompeii and all the people in it!"

"Quiet, slave! Did someone instruct you to talk?

You are not to speak unless you are spoken to."

The woman hustled them out of the cell and into Via dell'Abbondanza. Two angry-looking guards armed with spears were waiting there, so escaping was out of the question.

"Where do you think they're taking us?" Isabel whispered to Julia as they were escorted down the busy street.

"I don't care," Julia replied. "Nothing could be worse than being chained up in that dungeon. Maybe they're going to take us to one of those bathhouses. The Romans were famous for their baths, you know."

That was true. In fact, it's been said that the Romans built aqueducts so the people would have fresh water to take baths. Cleanliness, as they say, is next to godliness. There were three bathhouses in Pompeii.

But the girls were not being taken to the baths.

They were marched down Via dell'Abbondanza and made a left at Via Stabiana, passing a bakery and a shop that sold leather goods. As they turned the corner, Isabel caught a glimpse of Mount Vesuvius in the distance. It still looked quiet and peaceful.

Julia noticed the large clay jugs on the ground in front of many of the shops. She remembered Miss Z had talked about them. Then she saw a man walk up to one of the jugs and start peeing into it.

"That is so *gross!*" she told Isabel, pointing at the man. "Do you see that? Don't they have bathrooms here?"

"Quiet, slaves!" barked the woman leading them. "Let's go. In here. It is time."

"Huh?" Isabel said, as they approached one of the larger storefronts. "Time for what?"

"Time for you to *work*," the woman said, opening the door. "You will work in the fullery."

"Fullery?" Julia whispered to Isabel. "I don't know what that means. What's a fullery?"

"No clue."

"I thought you were the smart one."

The sign above the front door said—in Latin— "Fullonica Stephani." Or Stephen's Fullery.

"You will like it here," the woman told Julia and Isabel. "The work is easy, and Stephen is a good man."

"And what if we don't *want* to work?" asked Julia.

"Slaves who do not work are put to death," the woman said, quite matter-of-factly. "It would be wise to cooperate with Stephen."

Inside, the shop had beautiful tile mosaics on the

floor and impressive garden scenes painted on the walls. It looked like a lovely place, actually, and the girls relaxed just a little. Maybe working in the fullery wouldn't be too bad while they figured out a way to escape.

The shop was mostly filled with sheets and clothes hanging up on clotheslines. Behind the counter was a heavyset shopkeeper—Stephen—and what appeared to be his customer, a short woman holding a large cloth sack. She dumped a load of clothing onto the counter.

"I need these back by Saturday," the woman told Stephen.

"No problem, Mrs. Horatia."

"I guess a fullery is like a laundromat," Isabel whispered to Julia.

Isabel was right. And as Miss Z had informed them, clean clothes were important to the Romans.

"We have to work in a laundromat?"

"There are a lot *worse* places they could make us work," Isabel whispered. "They could force us to clean out toilets."

The customer left and Stephen came out from behind the counter.

"I see you have new slaves for me," he said cheerfully to the woman who had brought the girls there.

"Good, good! I need both of them immediately. We are backed up with work."

He gave the woman a handful of coins. She thanked him and left.

"Come with me, slaves," Stephen said.

He summoned a guard with a spear to accompany him as he led the girls through a hallway to another room.

"This shouldn't be too bad," Julia whispered. "How hard could it be to clean clothes?"

"They don't have washing machines, you know," Isabel whispered back. "They can't just throw their clothes in, add detergent, and push a button."

"Maybe they beat the clothes against rocks or something," Julia guessed. "Isn't that how they cleaned clothes in the old days?"

"As soon as they're not looking, let's make a run for it, okay?" Isabel whispered.

"I'm with you."

"What are you two whispering about, slaves?" asked Stephen.

"Nothing."

The guard holding the spear looked at girls suspiciously. He was going to keep a close eye on them.

"Welcome to my fullery," Stephen said, spreading

his arms wide when they reached the entrance to a large room. Clearly, he was proud of the business he had built.

The walls were red and decorated with fantastic paintings of birds and animals. There were more colorful mosaics on the floor. In the corner was a large machine that looked a little like an old-time printing press, but was actually a primitive clothes dryer. You would put wet clothes into it, and then turn a screw to squeeze the water out.

"I have other business to attend to," Stephen told the girls. Then he addressed the guard. "Marcellus, put these slaves to work."

Stephen left, and the guard he called Marcellus pointed to a large square tub in the middle of the room. It was about the size of a playground sandbox, and filled about three-quarters of the way up with some kind of liquid.

"Ugh, it smells like somebody peed in here," Julia said, holding her nose.

"I think somebody *did* pee in here," Isabel replied.

At that moment, another slave girl came in with a large clay jug and poured the yellow contents into the tub.

"Ugh, gross!" exclaimed Julia. "It's full of *pee*!"

"Get to work, slaves," said Marcellus the guard.

"What do you want us to do?" Isabel asked.

"Step on it," he replied.

"Huh?"

The girls thought that maybe their Ear Buddies were malfunctioning. Or maybe Marcellus was joking.

"You are to trod in the tub," he said, raising his voice. "Idiots! Have you never worked in a fullery before?"

The girls looked inside the tub more closely. There were clothes floating in the urine.

"Wait, you expect us to walk around in *that*?" Julia asked.

"Yes."

"Walk around in the *pee*?" added Isabel. She couldn't believe it.

"Yes!" Marcellus said, a little more insistently. "To get the dirt out."

"And the clothes are soaking in *pee*?" asked Julia.

"Yes! Of course!"

It seemed incomprehensible to the girls, but it was true. Urine has a lot of nitrogen in it. When it sits for a week or so, it becomes a rich source of ammonia, which is good for cleaning. That's why the clay jugs were placed in front of storefronts all over Pompeii—for people to fill up with urine.

"Are you *kidding* me?" Julia asked Marcellus. "You clean your clothes with . . . urine?"

"Of course," he replied. "What do they do with urine where *you* come from?"

"We flush it down the toilet," Julia told him. "Duh!"

"That is a waste of good urine," said Marcellus. "It removes the grease, oils, dirt, and other impurities. One man's waste is another man's treasure."

"Well, I'm not putting *my* feet into a tub of pee," Julia said. "That's just crazy. Come on, Isabel. Let's go. We don't need this."

She was prepared to march out in a huff, but Marcellus pulled a knife from his belt, grabbed Julia from behind, and held the knife against her neck.

"Perhaps you would rather have your throat sliced open?" he asked. "That's what we do to uncooperative slaves."

"Okay! Okay!" Julia shouted, her eyes bulging out in fear.

"Let her go!" screamed Isabel.

Marcellus let Julia go. The girls stepped onto the edge of the tub, holding up their frocks so they wouldn't get wet.

"Are you *sure* you don't have any laundry detergent?" Julia asked hopefully. "Some Tide, maybe?"

"There are tides in the ocean," replied Marcellus.

"A little soap?"

"Soap?" said Marcellus. "Why would Stephen pay good money for soap when urine is free?"

"Can't argue with that," Isabel said as she hesitantly dipped a toe into the urine. Reluctantly, Julia did the same.

"I can't believe I'm doing this," Julia said, holding her nose.

"This is the most disgusting thing I have ever done in my life," Isabel said as she put her whole foot into the tub. "I may pass out."

"I *hope* I pass out," Julia told her. "Then I won't have to smell it anymore."

"Move your feet around, slaves!" instructed Marcellus. "Circulate the urine."

Slowly, the girls moved their feet back and forth in the tub.

"Think of it this way," Isabel reasoned. "The pee is usually *inside* our bodies, right? That doesn't gross us out. Now it's just *outside* our bodies."

"I'm still grossed out," Julia replied. "I would rather clean out a toilet than *stand* in one!"

"Keep moving, slaves!" shouted Marcellus. "The clothes do not clean themselves!"

Totally disgusted, the girls marched around in the urine, being careful not to let their frocks dip below the surface. Actually, after doing that for a few minutes, they got used to the smell so it didn't bother them as much.

"Excuse me, how long do we have to do this?" Isabel asked.

"Two hours," replied Marcellus.

"What?!" Julia exclaimed. "I've got news for you, sir. In less than two hours, Mount Vesuvius is going to erupt and this whole town will be buried in ash."

"Shut up, slave!"

So this is where we are, reader. Things were not going very well for the Flashback Four. While Luke was fighting for his life against Vulcan, the girls were walking around in a tub full of pee. While David was running from the hungry tiger, the girls were *still* walking around in a tub full of pee. Soon Mount Vesuvius was going to erupt and kill everybody.

Other than that, things were fine.

* * *

"We've *got* to get out of here," Julia whispered to Isabel as they tromped around in the tub. "Then we've got to find the boys."

Isabel looked up to see Marcellus pacing back and forth around the big room.

"Do you have a plan?" she whispered to Julia.

"See that door near the corner? As soon as Marcellus turns his back, let's make a run for it."

Isabel glanced at the door.

"If he catches us, he'll kill us," she whispered.

"We've got to try *something*," Julia said. "We're going to die if we stay here."

"Okay, okay," Isabel whispered. "Next time he walks over to the far corner, we go."

They watched out of the corners of their eyes as Marcellus paced around the room. He made his way over to the far corner, the one that was farthest from the door.

"Now!" Julia whispered.

But before they could make a move, the door opened. It was Stephen, the owner of the fullery. He strode over to them.

"Ah, I see you have done good work, slaves," he told the girls. "Now it is time for you to dye."

"What?!" Julia shouted. "You're going to kill us?"

"We stomped in the pee like we were told!" Isabel yelled. "What *more* do you want from us? Please don't kill us!"

"We'll do anything!" Julia hollered. "We don't want to die!"

"Not die, idiots!" shouted Stephen. "Dye! It is time for you to dye the cloth."

"Oh. Never mind."

The Ear Buddy, apparently, did not understand homonyms.

CHAPTER 18

THE MAIN EVENT

DOWN THE ROAD, IN THE AMPHITHEATER, DAVID was on his knees, desperately trying save the life of the tiger he had accidentally stabbed in the heart.

"Nooooooo!" he kept wailing. "It was a *mistake*! I didn't mean to kill him! Is there a veterinarian in the house?"

It was very doubtful that there was a veterinarian in the house. And even if there *was* a veterinarian in the house, the veterinarian would probably be rooting for the tiger to die. In any case, it wasn't going to be saved. It had already lost too much blood.

"I killed it!" David wailed. "I can't believe I killed it!"

The crowd, of course, was eating it up. David put on a great show for them, and he wasn't even trying. People were yelling, screaming, and chanting his name.

"Hilarius! Hilarius! Hilarius!"

Finally the gate was opened, and Fred the Red came over to pull the grief-stricken boy away from the dying tiger. He handed David a palm branch of victory and put a laurel crown on his head. Then he escorted him back to the Palestra Grande. The crowd was still on its feet.

Luke was waiting for David. He saw how upset he was, and put his arms around his friend to comfort him.

"It's okay, man."

"I *killed* him," David sobbed, "and tigers are on the endangered species list!"

"If you hadn't killed him, *you'd* be on the endangered species list," Luke told him. "You won, and you survived! That's the most important thing."

"I don't want to live anymore," David said, still crying. "I'll have to live with the guilt."

"Look, it was *my* fault," Luke told him. "I never should have mentioned the bat flip idea."

"But now he's dead," David said, unable to control

himself. "It will be on my conscience *forever.*"

Luke wasn't getting through to his friend. At that point, he knew he had to resort to desperate measures. So he slapped David in the face.

"There isn't gonna *be* a forever!" he shouted at his friend. "We gotta figure a way out of here right *now.* What's done is done. So pull yourself together, dude!"

David pulled himself together. A slap in the face will do that to you. He pulled the timer out of his pocket.

"We have twenty-three minutes left."

At that point, Fred the Red came over to them. He had a big smile on his face.

"Slaves!" he said, putting one arm around each of the boys. "Both of you were *incredible* out there! I can hardly believe you boys are still alive. Congratulations. Come with me."

"Which one?" David asked.

"Both."

"Both of us?" asked Luke.

"Yes! Oceanus and Hilarius. Both of you! Come with me."

In the background, alternating chants were ringing from the crowd. They wouldn't stop.

"Hilarius! Hilarius! Hilarius!"

"Oceanus! Oceanus! Oceanus!"

"Do you hear that?" asked Fred the Red as he walked them toward the gate again. "The citizens of Pompeii love you."

"I guess they want us to take a bow," David said to Luke. "Like, a curtain call."

"You were both victorious," Fred the Red said. "So now, of course, you must fight against each other."

It took a moment for those words to sink in.

"Wait, what?" Luke asked. "But we're friends. We can't fight each other."

"Do you hear that chanting?" asked Fred the Red. "You must prove which one is the ultimate champion. The citizens demand it."

"No," David told him firmly. "We're friends. We don't fight each other."

The smile vanished from Fred the Red's face.

"You are friends who will *fight*," he insisted. "Or would you rather I send you out there with no weapons and simply release the lions? That would also be enjoyable to the crowd."

David looked at Luke. Luke flashed him a wink and put his helmet on.

"Let's go," he said. "If they want a show, we'll give 'em a show."

David put his helmet on. Both boys were handed identical shields and long swords.

"May the better man win," said Fred the Red as the gate was raised once again.

The guy with the megaphone quickly made an announcement.

"Citizens of Pompeii! And now . . . a special treat. The victors Oceanus and Hilarius will face each other in battle. A battle . . . to the *death*!"

A huge roar greeted Luke and David as they walked through the gate again.

"Oceanus! Oceanus! Oceanus!"

"Hilarius! Hilarius! Hilarius!"

The boys took a bow. The gate closed behind them.

"What do we do *now*?" David whispered as they walked slowly out to the middle of the arena. "What's the plan?"

"The plan is we fake it," Luke whispered back, "just like they do in pro wrestling. I beat you up for two minutes. Then you beat me up for two minutes. We fight to a draw, and they crown us. Then we figure out how to ditch this place before we run out of time."

A hush fell over the crowd as the boys faced off against one another in the middle of the arena. They circled each other cautiously, and then Luke suddenly charged at David, swinging his sword wildly. David retreated as he fended off Luke's weak blows with his shield.

"Good!" Luke said as he swung the sword low and David jumped over it. "You're really selling it!"

His back almost against the wall, David then went on the attack. The sword felt good in his hand, so much better than that silly trident he had to use against the tiger. He was slashing it around the way he'd seen fencers do it in the movies, almost hitting Luke a few times by accident. Neither boy actually wanted to hurt the other one. They just wanted to put on a good show.

"Booooooo!"

The crowd wasn't buying it. People started throwing stuff into the arena. These were sophisticated fans. They had been to enough competitions to know when a gladiator was trying his hardest and when he was just going through the motions.

Booooor-ring!

Luke and David stopped and turned around. Four big guards with spears had come out. They were marching toward the boys.

"Fight, slaves!" one of them instructed.

"We *are* fighting!" Luke replied.

212

"Fight with enthusiasm," the guard said. "Your friendship is admirable. But the citizens demand your blood. And your blood will be spilled . . . one way or another."

The guards surrounded the boys and raised their spears.

"Kill them both!" chanted the crowd. "Kill them both!"

"So, what's Plan B?" David asked Luke.

While Luke was desperately trying to come up with another plan, the guards backed away. Somebody else had come out of the gate. It was the guy dressed as Mercury, the Roman god of war. He was carrying his red-hot poker.

"Oh *no*," said Luke. "Not *this* guy again."

"Are you going to fight?" Mercury asked when he reached the middle of the arena. "Or will you continue this little dance? What's it gonna be, boys? Yes or no?"

Mercury thrust the glowing poker so it was just inches from Luke's face.

Luke backed away. He looked at the guards surrounding him with spears, and then at the angry crowd. There was no way out. The timer was clicking down. He had run out of options. There was no Plan

B. His optimism was gone. His shoulders sagged. He sighed.

"I think it's all over for us, David," he said sadly. "It's finished."

"What's it gonna be?" asked Mercury.

"We will fight," Luke replied. "For real."

"You have made a wise decision," said one of the guards.

The timer counted down: 17 minutes.

"So that's it?" David asked, incredulous. *"That's* your Plan B? We fight for *real,* until one of us is dead?"

"Look," Luke told his friend. "There's no way outta here. The mountain's gonna blow any minute and we're gonna die anyway. So we might as well go out in a blaze of glory, right? I know you've wondered which one of us would win in a fight. So have I. Well, let's find out."

David was stunned. He didn't know if he would be capable of hurting Luke, who had become his best friend in the time they had been together. But he had learned something from Luke—there was one weapon that was incredibly powerful against any opponent— the element of surprise.

Instead of squaring off like two fighters usually do, David quickly swung his sword as hard as he could at

Luke's head before Luke could put his shield up.

Instinctively, Luke ducked, with David's sword passing less than an inch from his nose.

The crowd roared in appreciation. *Now* they had a show to watch.

Luke reeled backward and fell to the dirt. When his right hand hit the ground, he lost the grip on his sword. It slid a few feet away. David pounced like a cat, taking a big roundhouse swing at Luke. Luke ducked and spun out of the way, moving quite fast for a big boy. Of course, *you'd* move pretty fast too if somebody was swinging a razor-sharp sword at you.

"Nice try!" Luke said as he grabbed his sword again and jumped up off the ground. "But too slow."

Now it was Luke's turn, using his weight and strength advantage to drive David backward, shoving him roughly with his shield. David staggered, but then righted himself.

"You're not playing around, are you?" Luke asked as he slashed at David with his sword. David blocked it, making a loud metal clang. "Well, neither am I."

While the boys were flailing away at each other, few people in the crowd noticed that all the birds had disappeared from the sky. A few dogs were barking and sniffing the air curiously. Animals have senses that pick up signals we can't receive. There was an eerie silence, a stillness in the air. The ground had begun to vibrate.

And then, Mount Vesuvius erupted.

BOOM!

CHAPTER 19

RUN FOR YOUR LIFE

IT WAS AN INDESCRIBABLE DOUBLE CRACK OF sound, a thunderous explosion unlike any noise David or Luke had ever heard before. It was unlike any noise *anybody* had ever heard before, or since. The energy released when Mount Vesuvius erupted, historians say, was *a hundred thousand times* the force of the atomic bomb that destroyed Hiroshima to end World War II. That's how loud the blast was.

Luke and David dropped their swords and shields immediately so they could cover their ears and protect their eardrums from being ripped to shreds.

Everyone in the amphitheater did the same. All heads turned toward the north, where the sound was coming from. It was impossible to see Mount Vesuvius from the inside of the amphitheater, so it was unclear what was going on. The only people there who knew exactly what had happened were Luke and David.

"Ahhhhhhhhhh!"

"It's happening!"

It wasn't just one quick blast, like a typical explosion. It was a long, continuous roar that went on and on. Keep in mind, the people of Pompeii had never been to a *Star Wars* film. They'd never heard a bomb go off. They'd never seen a car explode in the movies. This was something *completely* different for them.

Just a moment earlier, every man, woman, and child in the crowd had been riveted by the spectacle of Oceanus and Hilarius fighting to the death. But a moment after the blast, not a single one of those people cared about the gladiators.

"What's happening?" everyone was asking.

"The gods must be furious!" was the general response.

In these ancient times, anything that happened, for good or for bad, was believed to be caused by the gods. If the people pleased the gods, they would be rewarded. If they displeased the gods, they would be punished. That was what they believed. So when they heard the explosion, they figured somebody must have done something *really* bad.

But whatever they had done to displease the gods, there was nothing they could do about it now. The place went into full-scale panic mode.

Guards dropped their swords and abandoned their posts. Food vendors dropped what they were selling. Children started crying. The caged animals were squawking and bucking. Old people, young people, men and women started running for the exits. All the slaves were suddenly free men and women.

"It is the end of the world!" somebody screamed.

Luke and David looked around for a moment at the commotion. This was just the opposite of what they had experienced on the *Titanic*, where it had taken two hours for the ship to sink. The panic had built very gradually. But Vesuvius was sudden and dramatic. Everybody knew right away that something was terribly wrong.

Fred the Red was nowhere to be seen. He had already made a run for it, heading out of the city. The other guards were gone too. The timer counted down. They had fourteen minutes to get to the meeting spot.

"Let's go!" Luke shouted to David over the roar of noise. "This is our chance!"

The boys helped each other scale the arena wall and climb into the stands. From there, they scrambled past some old men wearing togas and pushed their way to the exit.

In the Fullonica Stephani, Isabel and Julia were dipping some shirts into red dye under Stephen's watchful eye when the volcano erupted.

BOOM!

"What in the Underworld is *that*?" Stephen shouted, covering his ears.

"It's Mount Vesuvius!" Isabel yelled at him. "It's erupting!"

In a flash, Stephen was out on the street. The guards in the fullery left their posts too. Nobody was watching the girls.

"Let's go!" Isabel shouted into Julia's ear, the only way she could be heard over the noise.

The girls dashed out to the street, which was filled with people, animals, and carts going every which way, crashing into each other. Isabel led the way to a street called Via della Fortuna. A bunch of people were standing on the corner there, staring off into the distance.

"Look!" Isabel shouted, pointing at Vesuvius.

The top of the mountain was gone. Above it, a black mushroom cloud was rising.

Meanwhile, in Boston, Miss Z and Mrs. Vader were nervous and worried. They had not heard from the Flashback Four for a long time. They didn't know that the TTT had been destroyed, so they had no idea what the kids were going through. Miss Z had made the very difficult decision to wait until the agreed-upon time— fifteen minutes after noon—to bring them back.

If something had gone wrong and the Flashback Four weren't at the meeting spot at twelve fifteen, they would be stuck in Pompeii for the rest of lives. Their very *short* lives. And Miss Z would be held responsible for their disappearance, of course.

"Nine minutes left," Mrs. Vader said, looking at her watch.

"By now, they should have taken the picture of Mount Vesuvius," said Miss Z. "They should be at the meeting spot for us to scoop them up."

"I'll warm up the Board," said Mrs. Vader.

* * *

But the Flashback Four had *not* taken the picture of Vesuvius, and they were *not* at the meeting spot. They weren't even together. The girls were standing at the corner of Via della Fortuna and Via del Foro, staring up at the sky with a few hundred other people. They all stared, transfixed, at a thick brown line that was shooting straight up from the top of Mount Vesuvius. It looked like the mountain was punching a hole in the sky.

There's no word in Latin for volcano. Most of the citizens of Pompeii didn't even know that Vesuvius *was* a volcano. It hadn't erupted in eight hundred years. But it didn't take a genius to realize this was an "earthshaking" event.

"The sleeping giant has awoken," an old man said. "Pray for us."

Meanwhile, Luke and David were still eight blocks to the west, elbowing their way through the hordes of confused, frantic people trying to make a getaway. The streets were clogged and almost impassable. A horse reared, throwing off its rider and trampling a woman who had fallen down. Shrieking. Crying. Chaos. Most of the people had no idea what was going on.

"Is it another earthquake?" an old woman asked. Only the adults of Pompeii remembered the quake in the year 62, which had just about reduced the town to rubble.

"Five minutes," Miss Z said in Boston, checking her watch. Let's get ready."

The column of dark smoke and ash continued to shoot out of Mount Vesuvius and spread across the sky. It was already getting darker as the flying debris began to obscure the sun. If anyone had stopped and held a finger in the air, they would have been able to tell that the wind was blowing south, directly toward Pompeii.

People were hurrying in all directions with boxes, bags, and trunks. It was a mass of confusion as everyone was fighting to grab their jewels and worldly possessions. Some were heading for the Bay of Naples a quarter of a mile away, where they might be able to escape on a boat.

Shopkeepers rushed to carry their wares off the street and bring them inside. Looters grabbed what they could from stores. Children were separated from their parents and called out for them. Frightened dogs and other animals strained to break free of their leashes. Statues were knocked off their pedestals by wayward carts, shattering as they hit the ground. People were limping, crying, bleeding.

For once, the rich and poor people of Pompeii were equal. It didn't matter anymore how much money or how many possessions anyone owned. They had lived separate lives, but they were going to die together.

"The gods are merciless!" somebody shouted.

"They have decided to kill us all!"

David and Luke ran through the streets like fullbacks, trying to make their way to the Porta Marina gate. But so were hundreds of others. The boys came to an intersection filled with people, horses, and goats.

"Which way should we go?" David asked, looking around frantically.

"Follow me!" Luke shouted.

"Two minutes," Miss Z said in Boston.

The citizens of Pompeii realized that all the rock, ash, and debris shooting out of Mount Vesuvius was going to hit the ground eventually. Even in the year 79, people knew that what goes up must come down.

In fact, pieces of pumice had already started falling from the sky. Pumice is a gray stone that has little holes in it, like a sponge. It's so light that it floats in water. But it hurts when it lands on you. Some people took shelter in doorways. Others ran through the street holding pillows over their heads to protect themselves. Still others cowered in their homes, hoping the whole thing was going to blow over in a few minutes. Big mistake.

"The city will be buried!" a bleeding man shouted as he ran through the street.

Julia and Isabel managed to push and claw their way toward the Porta Marina gate.

"This way!" Isabel shouted, pointing to the spot a few feet from the gate where they had arrived two hours earlier.

Coming from the other direction, David and Luke were almost there too.

"One minute," Miss Z said in Boston.

The Flashback Four dashed through the Porta Marina gate at almost at the same moment.

"Luke!" shouted Julia.

"Isabel!" shouted David.

"Julia!" shouted Luke.

"David!" shouted Isabel.

Group hug.

"Ugh, you two smell *terrible!*" David said. "Did you pee in your pants or something?"

"Hey, you guys don't smell so great yourselves," said Julia.

"You won't *believe* what we've been through!" Isabel told the boys.

"Oh, you won't believe what *we've* been through," Luke told the girls.

David looked at the timer. It was flashing 1 minute.

"We can talk about it later," he shouted. "Let's go. Over here."

The Flashback Four ran to the meeting spot. The only problem was that a teenage boy was standing there. He was looking off in the distance, trying to locate his friends.

"Excuse me," Isabel said politely. "We need to be at this spot."

The boy looked at her with disdain.

"Who died and made *you* emperor?" he replied.

"I'm standing here now."

Luke and David went up to the teenager. Without missing a beat, Luke punched him in the stomach and David smacked him over the head.

"Beat it!" Luke said as the guy doubled over and staggered away.

"Where did you guys learn to fight like that?" Julia asked as they took the boy's place.

"We'll tell you later," Luke said. "Gather around."

The Flashback Four squeezed together, their arms around each other.

"Let's hope Miss Z didn't forget about us," Isabel said as a piece of pumice landed on the ground in front of her. She closed her eyes in preparation for going back home.

"Okay, let's do it," Miss Z said, sitting at her computer in Boston. "Cross your fingers."

She hit the ENTER key to activate the Board.

The timer flashed 0 minutes.

"Wait!" Luke said suddenly. "I forgot something!"

"What!?" David shouted. "We're out of time!"

Luke reached into his pocket for the camera, which

was still in one piece, miraculously, after all Luke had been through.

"Oh yeah, the picture!" shouted David.

Luke quickly pointed the camera at Mount Vesuvius. It was hard to hold it steady with all the confusion around them and pumice falling from the sky. But Luke managed to push the button and get off one shot.

Right after he took the picture, Luke looked up and saw the teenager that he and David had just beaten up. He was running toward them, and he had four friends with him. They looked like a street gang. They had long sticks in their hands.

The Board flashed five bands of color, which merged into one high-intensity strobe light that flickered a few feet off the Board like miniature bolts of lightning.

"Over there!" the angry teenager said, pointing at the Flashback Four.

"Are those the guys who punched you?" one of his gang asked.

"Yeah, that's them. The two boys."

They were only a few feet away.

"When you hit one of us, you hit *all* of us," one of the guys said.

He raised his stick. The others did the same. The Flashback Four put their hands up to protect their faces.

A humming, crackling sound filled the air. A powerful invisible force froze the Flashback Four.

"So long, suckers!" shouted David.

And then they vanished.

"Where did they go?" one of the gang asked.

An instant later, the Flashback Four appeared in the office of Pasture Company in Boston, Massachusetts. They landed on the floor, gasping for breath, happy, relieved, exhausted, and emotional.

"You're back!" shouted Mrs. Vader, rushing over to greet the kids. "We were getting a little worried about you."

Luke, Julia, Isabel, and David got up from the floor and brushed themselves off.

"So," Miss Z said excitedly. "Tell us what happened! Did everything go according to plan? How was Pompeii?"

"Did anything exciting happen?" asked Mrs. Vader. "Did you encounter any problems?"

"Problems?" asked Luke. "No! No problems at all!"

The Flashback Four looked at each other and burst out laughing.

EPILOGUE

WHAT WILL HAPPEN TO THE FLASHBACK FOUR *next*? Will they ever recover from their adventure in Pompeii? Is their time-traveling career finally over for good?

You'll have to wait for Flashback Four #4 to find out!

FACTS & FICTIONS

Everything in this book is true, except for the stuff I made up. It's only fair to tell you which is which.

First, the made-up stuff. The Flashback Four, Miss Z, and Mrs. Vader do *not* exist. They are fictional characters. (But Hilarius was a real name in Roman times. It meant "cheerful.") There's no such thing as a smart-board that enables people to travel through time. And there's no TTT to send texts through time or an Ear Buddy to translate foreign languages. At least not yet.

Most of the other stuff is true. To research this book I visited Pompeii to see it with my own eyes, and I also watched videos, scanned websites, and read many other books on the subject. To name a few: *The Fires of Vesuvius*, by Mary Beard; *Bodies from the Ash*, by James M. Deem; *Pompeii: Lost & Found*, by Mary Pope Osborne; *The Buried City of Pompeii*, by Shelley Tanaka; *The Lost City of Pompeii*, by Dorothy Hinshaw

Patent; *Pompeii*, by Richard Platt; and *Pompeii*, by Robert Harris.

The descriptions of ancient and present-day Pompeii were pretty much accurate. Fullonica Stephani was a real laundry. And yes, the laundries of that time period actually used urine to clean the clothes. It is true that slaves were used to stomp around in tubs full of pee.

In fact, that's only one of *many* uses of urine. Throughout history, people have used the stuff for softening leather, making gunpowder, and—are you ready for this?—toothpaste and mouthwash! It's true! Until the eighteenth century, urine was one of the most common ingredients in mouthwash. Don't believe me? Look it up for yourself.

The Pompeii amphitheater, Palestra Grande, and the gladiator games were very much the way they were described, but even more bloody and gruesome. Hey, this is a book for kids! If you want to read *all* the gory details, well, that's why they invented Google.

When Pompeii was finally unearthed, the skeletons of eighteen men and one horse were found at the Palestra Grande, where the gladiators trained. Historians have estimated that there were about four hundred amphitheaters like this throughout the Roman Empire, and as many as eight thousand gladiators died in them each year.

Finally, of course, Mount Vesuvius is a real volcano that buried Pompeii—and the nearby town of Herculaneum—in the year 79. The volcano has erupted numerous times since then, including in 1872, when the photo that appears on page 228 was taken. To this day it is an active volcano, and three million people live a short distance away from it around the Bay of Naples.

It could blow again at any time.

ABOUT THE AUTHOR

Besides Flashback Four, Dan Gutman is the author of several other series—The Genius Files, My Weird School, Rappy the Raptor, the Baseball Card Adventures—as well as many other books for young readers. He lives in New York City with his wife, Nina. You can find out more about Dan and his books at www.dangutman.com.

ALSO BY
DAN GUTMAN

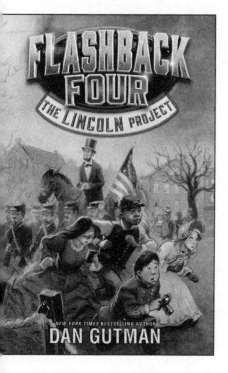

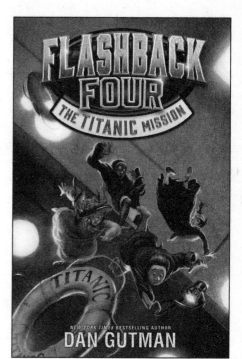

A TIME-TRAVELING ADVENTURE UNLIKE ANY OTHER!

HARPER
n Imprint of HarperCollinsPublishers

www.harpercollinschildrens.com

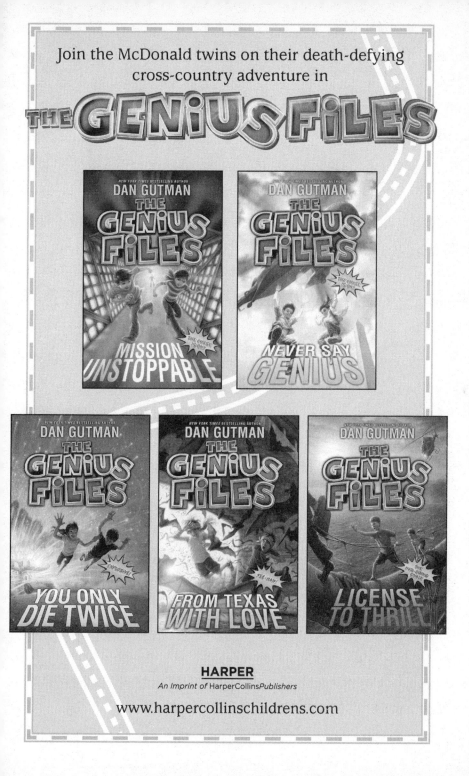